Gina,
I ho
book too!

Fong

New Land
Same Sky

a novel

C FONG HSIUNG

MAWENZI
HOUSE

©2018 C Fong Hsiung

Except for purposes of review, no part of this book may be reproduced in any form without prior permission of the publisher.

We acknowledge the support of the Canada Council for the Arts for our publishing program. We also acknowledge support from the Government of Ontario through the Ontario Arts Council.

ONTARIO ARTS COUNCIL
CONSEIL DES ARTS DE L'ONTARIO
an Ontario government agency
un organisme du gouvernement de l'Ontario

Canada Council   Conseil des arts
for the Arts   du Canada

Cover designed by Sabrina Pignataro

Cover photo: Ditty_about_summer/travel concept, people in the airport/ Shutterstock

Library and Archives Canada Cataloguing in Publication

Hsiung, C. Fong, author
New land same sky : a novel / C Fong Hsiung.

Issued in print and electronic formats.
ISBN 978-1-988449-46-3 (softcover).--ISBN 978-1-988449-47-0 (HTML)

    I. Title.

PS8615.S58N49 2018   C813'.6   C2018-904832-8
                                       C2018-904833-6

Mawenzi House Publishers Ltd.
39 Woburn Avenue (B)
Toronto, Ontario M5M 1K5
Canada

www.mawenzihouse.com

"Run away with me, Maylei," Keith pleads.

"Marry me," says Wen-Lung.

I put my hands to my ears and scream, "Stop it, both of you."

My heart palpitates and I find it hard to sleep; at times I drift off into a state where I'm not sure if I've been awake or dreaming. My womb stirs—a flutter reminding me of the life growing inside me. I touch the growing bulge below my naval and send silent messages down: "Hello there, what's keeping you awake?" I turn to my side and reach out for Jay-Son and wrap an arm around his little body. He thrashes his arms and moans. Behind me Wen-Lung lets out periodic snores. I sigh and resist the urge to nudge him. He has a long day ahead of him.

The ceiling fan whirring above me is not enough to cool me, and I stick my feet out under the cotton sheet. Jay-Son's body feels hot on my arm, and sweat tickles my breasts. I hear Wen-Lung wheeze before his breath motors on. It's hard to believe that he will leave us in less than twenty-four hours. Canada beckoned and we could not resist.

❖ ❖ ❖

My mind wanders . . . Earlier, Mrs Yang from a few houses down came tearing up, hair flying, screaming in Hakka, "Help, help . . . please help! Yun-Ti . . . my husband. He's hurt. Thieves . . . bad men . . . help."

I got up from the concrete bench on which I'd been sitting

outside the tannery and rushed towards her, as fast as my swelling belly allowed. I grasped her hands. "What happened?"

She sobbed, "Yun-Ti . . . he, ah . . . lots of blood . . . tied to chair."

I led her to the bench. Between tears and gulps, she told me how she had returned from visiting her parents to find her husband bound to a chair with ropes. Blood all over his face and body. Mr Yang said Indian thugs had attacked him while he was napping. They made off with money and gold jewelry. He was alone in his tannery that hot afternoon, when most residents of Tangra would have been away from their homes, many to central Calcutta for the Sunday matinee at air-conditioned movie theaters. This was a brazen act in the heart of our Hakka Chinese neighborhood.

I dismiss these distressing mental pictures and tell myself that with lots of hard work and luck, we will leave all this behind us. Wen-Lung is right to go to Canada. He will send for us as soon as he becomes a permanent resident there.

Still, my mind continues to wander. The previous night, Mok-Shin Wong, Wen-Lung's employer and the owner of the tannery where we live, had invited Wen-Lung and me to visit him in his room, next to the tannery's front door. He pulled out a long wooden case from under his king-size bed, inserted a key into a small padlock and lifted the lid. He pulled a red velvet covering aside to reveal a rifle. His moon-face crinkled in many places as he lifted his head to look at Wen-Lung. "The Yangs should get one of these. If those thieves ever attack us, they'll have to face this bad baby," he said in a booming voice.

I wondered whether Mr Yang could have reached the rifle—if he had one—in time to save himself. But Wen-Lung's dark brown eyes gleamed as he whispered, "Wow . . . do you know how to use it?"

Mok-Shin chuckled. "Of course, I do. The guy who sold it to

me let me fire it before I paid him."

It's almost fifteen years since the Sino-Indian War of 1962, and still, every now and then, Indian gangs come to steal or assault us here in Tangra, the leather-tanning district of Calcutta. Then for some days we talk of nothing but arming ourselves. The men pound their chests, and the women's mouths spew words like missiles that could surely kill these bad guys many times over.

I turn sideways to face Wen-Lung. His breathing sounds louder now that I'm facing him. I don't know when I'll see him again. I have both dreaded and looked forward to this parting. We decided when we got married two and a half years ago that we would immigrate to Canada as soon as possible. Our prospects here are limited—I, a local Chinese school teacher's second daughter and he, a small restaurant-owner's middle son. I work in a secretarial training school and Wen-Lung works as Mok-Shin's manager, supervising the leather workers. My parents could not afford to let me go to college after I completed high school in English, where I had been fortunate enough to be sponsored by an international charity. Wen-Lung had only finished Class Nine in English when Mok-Shin hired him.

We have skimped and saved so we can pay for our way out of India one day. Last year, our Canadian immigration application was rejected. Undaunted, and over my protests, Wen-Lung applied for a visitor's permit for himself. And miraculously he got it. With deep misgivings, I agreed to let him go on his own, but the timing couldn't be worse. Jay-Son will become a big brother soon after he turns two, in four months. I will give birth to a baby when my husband is in Toronto. Still, this could be our only chance to get into the land that has captured the Hakka imagination in our neighborhood.

Somehow I manage to snatch a few winks as I drift in and out of dreamland. Yes, we will leave this place one day. "Ching chong," the street urchins taunt us in sing-song voices. We will leave the violent clashes between hot-headed Chinese and Indian youths every time they look askance at each other. We will leave memories of the 1962 Sino-Indian Border Conflict and the repercussions we suffered; the mass arrests and detention of Indian Chinese, the travel restrictions on us, which were lifted only a few years ago. All in the past and yet still part of our everyday existence.

◆ ◆ ◆

I drag myself out of bed. I must get to the market place—open for a few hours only—and get back in time to go to work. I should have asked to take today off. Now it's too late, even though Mr Wilson, my boss at St Agnes' Secretarial School, would have agreed. Wen-Lung's flight will take off around midnight, but we plan to leave for the airport soon after dinner this evening. In the dark I find my way to the dresser, grope for my comb and quickly run it through my long hair, which I then tie back with an elastic band. I tuck my wallet inside the waist pocket of my cotton shirt and leave the room. I'm almost ready for the day.

From the top shelf of a cupboard containing my kitchen stuff at the back of the tannery, I grab a plastic mug with my toothbrush and toothpaste inside. I walk past the kitchen to reach the bathroom. Sliding the wooden bolt firmly into its slot, I lean back on the door to take a breath, then I sit down on the footstool there, and splash water on my face. The naked bulb on the ceiling casts a yellow hue on the unpainted cement walls. At this early hour the only sounds come from a crow cawing incessantly and the tuneless whistling of the night watchman. The impact of Wen-Lung's impending departure hits me like a blow. I swallow hard and start to retch. I breathe deeply until the nausea passes. Out of the bathroom, I unhook a wicker basket from the nail on the side of my kitchen cupboard and ease the handles onto the crook of my left arm. *"Darban, darwaja kholo,"* I call out in Hindi to the night watchman to open the door.

Used to my morning routine, he drops his truncheon on the floor and slides the massive wooden bar on the door to a side with surprising ease. He opens the door partly and I pass through the gap just large enough for me. By the time I return from the market, he will have opened the door all the way for the factory workers, supply vendors, and customers to move freely throughout the day. We live where we work, our rooms on one side of the tannery, merging seamlessly with the daily thrum of machines and all the tanning activities.

Yesterday's downpour—the first one this June—has waterlogged the potholed roads. Some of my Hakka neighbors swear that all the potholes in Calcutta have found their way to Tangra and become permanent residents. A glow lights up the eastern sky. The sun, starting to peek in the horizon behind the green fields across the ponds, seems to have chased away the thunderous clouds.

"Maylei, ah . . . wait for me," someone calls out in Hakka.

I stop and turn around. Pao-Chin Liu waddles up toward me, her wicker basket swaying beneath her fleshy arm. Panting, she says, "I just found out yesterday that your husband is going to Canada. Why so secretive, ah?" She heaves as she keeps pace, like me skirting by patches of mud and hopping over puddles.

Innocently I tell her, "I don't know what you mean. Wen-Lung has told his employer. His friends know too."

"I only just heard about it from my husband." Pao-Chin glances quickly around and lowers her voice. "Anyway, I wouldn't blame you if you want to keep this a secret. So many jealous people here, Maylei. You never know if someone will do something bad behind your back."

I wave a dismissive hand. "Oh, we're not worried about that."

I don't believe my own words because I've learned that we can never be too careful about what we say to our neighbors. This is especially true now, for Wen-Lung plans to stay in Toronto as an illegal immigrant. But I don't believe we have any enemies, and at some point in the future we will have to trust friends and acquaintances not to turn him in.

"So, will you continue to live in Mok-Shin's tannery?" she asks.

"Yes, there's no reason to move. Wen-Lung will be back in October before his ticket expires," I lie smoothly and wish it were true. "Since we've incurred such a huge expense for him to go to Canada, it only makes sense to stay for the full four months."

Pao-Chin stops to contemplate an extra-large puddle and raises her eyebrows. "Oh, I understand. Will he get back in time for your baby's birth?"

"Yes, he will."

I extend my arm to help Pao-Chin to cross, and then I change the topic. "Isn't it terrible what happened to Yun-Ti?"

"Tch, tch . . . These gangs are getting bolder nowadays. Imagine coming right into the house and beating the poor man in broad daylight."

"At least they didn't kill him. Do you remember how two goondas stabbed Sen-Chu last year when he was on his way home? He had just collected money from his customers. They stole every rupee he was carrying."

"Yes, he was very lucky to have survived the stabbing. His wife made many offerings at all the temples." Pao-Chin smirks. "I hear the Buddhist monks welcome her with open arms every time she visits."

The market square is buzzing with activity. Shoppers, mostly Hakka women, weave in and out among the vendors, who are mostly Indians. A butcher slices off pork parts with a cleaver on a table. Men and women entreat us with live chickens and vegetables. I part company with Pao-Chin and make my way towards a familiar figure sitting on the ground, presiding over piles of onions, tomatoes, and potatoes. Squatting down with some difficulty, I inspect her wares, ask for the prices. *"Kya dam hai,* Rani?"

Everyone calls her Rani, or Queen, and she's been a fixture in this place since before my birth. The end of her sari—draped loosely like a scarf over her head—falls down on her shoulders, her open mouth reveals large yellow and black teeth. We haggle a little and she tips my selections into my basket.

A curry begins to cook in my head as I heave myself up, and I turn around to look for other ingredients for the day's meals. Soon the vendors will pack up and the marketplace turn into a community center again.

"Maylei," a raspy voice says behind me. Suppressing a groan, I turn to face the speaker who was my matchmaker. "You are getting very big," she says, glancing at my stomach. "I hear that Wen—"

"Hello Mrs Lam, how is your daughter doing?"

A slight frown creases her brow at my inquiry, but then the lines disappear and her eyes soften. She's still basking in the after-glow of having become the proud grandmother of a nine-pound boy. She smiles and begins to describe in detail her daughter's marathon labor. I try to figure out how to make my getaway.

Finally, my shopping done, I make my departure, my basket creaking from the weight and its handles biting into one arm, and in the other hand a squawking chicken I hold by its feet. It's too expensive for our everyday meals, but worth the price for Wen-Lung's last meal with us. Until we see each other again. Behind me I hear someone say, "Yes, I heard that her husband is going to Canada tonight." Pao-Chin responds, "I only found out this morning."

· 2 ·

At eight-thirty I step on the pavement of Park Street, downtown, almost thrust out of a bus jammed with teeming, sweaty humanity. I breathe in deeply, stifle a cough and cross the street to the wrought-iron gate of the faded four-story building that houses St Agnes' School on its second floor, and businesses offices in the remaining spaces.

My boss is in the main lobby waiting for the lift. I wave and speak in English, "Hello, Mr Wilson."

Mr Wilson turns his pot-bellied figure towards me. "Ah, if it isn't Maylei Chen. Just the person I want to see this morning. So glad you're here early. I need to get an urgent letter out." The lopsided grin over a strong chin reminds me of someone else, much younger, and I push away the thought of Keith, his son. That episode with him is long over.

I continue towards the marble staircase—a dirty testament to past grandeur—in the middle of the lobby. "I'll meet you in the office, Mr Wilson!"

He casts a dubious glance at my belly. "Why don't you take the lift up with me?"

"I need to exercise the baby," I tell him, and grab the railing.

Richard Wilson, an Anglo-Indian, is the principal of the school. I took a nine-month program in typing and shorthand here soon after graduating from high school, after which Mr Wilson offered me the job as his secretary. This was sheer luck. Old Mrs Pinto, the former secretary, had just passed away, and I couldn't have been happier at landing a job without having to look for one.

As I settle into my chair in front of my typewriter, Mr Wilson lumbers in, wiping his face with a large handkerchief. "That Mohan takes his time with the lift. I swear he deliberately slows it down to annoy me."

I look up and chuckle. He says the same thing almost every morning, but every year he's the first person to give Mohan *baksheesh,* a generous tip, for Christmas. "I'm ready for your letter whenever you are," I tell him.

He drops his briefcase next to his desk, pulls out his chair and eases into it with a grunt. He wiggles the chair closer to his mahogany desk. "Let's get started." I grab a steno pad and pencil and join him at his desk. He holds up a document and clears his throat. "Dear Mr Gupta," he begins. Fifteen minutes later, after several tries, he says with a flourish, "Yours truly, Richard Wilson." He doesn't like this chore.

I push my chair back to rise, but he waves me back down. "When is your husband going to Canada?"

"Uh, tonight, actually."

He raises his eyebrows. "When's he coming back?"

"In about four months . . . "

"Does he really plan on returning to Calcutta?"

"Of course."

He snorts. "Maylei, I know what happens when young people go to Canada. They just don't bother coming back. Look at my son, remember him? He was lucky because he got his immigration papers before he left India. Not that I wanted him to go, but Keith always had a mind of his own." He added, "He'll get a good education, but . . . "

Keith. Of course I remember. Sometimes I wonder why I continue to work here, reminded of our break-up every time his father speaks his name.

"Wen-Lung wants to go and find out if Canada is the

right place for us."

Mr Wilson puffs an exasperated sigh. "I hope you young people know what you're doing. Your husband's place is with you right now, especially with your baby coming soon. Go home early today. Send off your husband properly."

He picks up a pen, looks down and begins to write in a notebook.

"Thank you, Mr Wilson."

I hurry back to type the letter. When I've finished, Mr Wilson has left, so I put it on top of his desk. There's his family photograph, taken the day Keith graduated from St Xavier's College. Not Chinese enough, that's why we parted. Part English, part Indian, and part Chinese. Not quite the right eyes, not the right hair. Not the right language. I was nineteen and he twenty-one.

As promised, Mr Wilson lets me off early and I leave the office at three. Half an hour later I step off the bus at the entrance to Tangra and walk on South Tangra Road. It is lined on both sides with some tanneries and mostly low-rise dwellings and stores. Many paths and trails branch out from this main street to a network of two hundred-plus tanneries.

The roadside gravel crunches below my sandaled feet. A lorry sputters past, spewing out black smoke into the atmosphere. Holding my handkerchief to my nose, I bump into a thela gadi piled high with furniture and get yelled at. I smile sheepishly at the driver. A wonderful aroma of spicy frying wafts toward me, and my mouth waters. I follow the smell to a stall selling fresh singaras, which I now know as samosas, and purchase a few. Shortly with a greasy newspaper bag in my hand, I turn into an unpaved path wide enough for one lorry or car and densely packed with tanneries on both sides. A few minutes later, the path forks. I take the one on my right and enter the tannery where our home is, to be greeted by an excited cry of, "Mama, mama!"

Jay-Son runs into my arms, a picture of joy, and I lift him up and kiss both his cheeks. Behind him, Didi says in Hindi, "Memsahib, you are home early."

I look past Jay-Son at our Nepalese maidservant. *Didi* means "elder sister." She's a small and wiry middle-aged woman, with a sparkling nose stud on one side of her sharp nose, which flares at the nostrils. Shadows lurk beneath her eyes, which I glimpse every time her drunken husband visits her in my kitchen.

"Yes, Didi, Wen-Lung *Sahib* is going away today. I'll take care of Jay-Son now. Please start the fire and then wash the rice. I'm cooking dinner early." Unlike the gas stove that Mok-Shin's wife Mrs Wong uses, I possess a clay stove, which takes longer to heat up.

Didi tilts her head to say, *"Achha, Memsahib."* She tucks the loose end of her faded sari at her waist and strides off purposefully towards the kitchen. Many Hakka women complain about their maids, but mine is perfect and I want to keep her as long as possible. She costs me a dear chunk of my salary, but she's worth it.

Wen-Lung looks up when he hears the door to our room close shut. His thin face looks ruddier than usual. "Maylei, oh, you're home."

I put Jay-Son down and the bag of fried singara on Wen-Lung's desk. His palms cup a steaming bowl of tea, his forearms rest on the desk. He looks at us with brooding eyes, and I wonder what he's thinking. Walking away to the cabinet beside the tall almirah with its double mirrored doors, I pick up the clay water pot there, and pour cold water into a plastic tumbler. I gulp down the water and knuckle away the wetness around my mouth.

"I see Didi has already made tea."

Wen-Lung puts a singara into his mouth, relishes the taste of fried pastry and curried potatoes. "I'm going to miss this when I'm gone."

Jay-Son has climbed up one of the two suitcases on the floor, strapped and ready to go with Wen-Lung tonight. He stands on top, flaps his arms, and jumps down to the floor. "Be careful!" I pick up a singara and finally sit down, across from my husband. A flutter like a feather grazes the inside of my middle bulge.

For a brief moment we watch Jay-Son's antics with the suitcase. Then Wen-Lung rubs his narrow chin and sighs. "I wonder when I will see you all again."

"It won't be long," I reply with feigned confidence. I go over the pile of clothes that Didi has neatly stacked on the bed and pick out a shirt and trousers, and stuff them inside the brown travel bag, a going-away gift from Mok-Shin and his wife made from their own leather. "We'll be together again soon. You'll find a way to stay in Canada, and then you'll sponsor us."

Why are we putting ourselves through this heartache? My gaze falls upon Jay-Son at play with the two suitcases. That's our reason.

"What if I can't find a job there? What am I trained to do besides factory work?"

"Don't talk like that. Gabriel will help you find work. He promised he would." Wen-Lung's best friend immigrated to Toronto a year ago and works as a welder in an auto parts factory.

Wen-Lung gets up from his chair and paces the floor, shoulders hunched, hands locked behind him. Moments later, he stops in front of the locked almirah, reaches into his trouser pocket, and pulls out a bunch of keys. "I've heard that many Hakka work in leather tanneries in Toronto. Maybe I too can find work in one of them. And when I've saved enough money, I'll apply for landed status. Others have done it, so I suppose I can do it too."

"Yes, you'll find work for sure. Ah-Sam told me that his older sister went to Canada on a visitor's permit, and she's already found work. You remember my friend, Joy, who trained as a secretary with me? She's been working in a factory for over a year despite having only a tourist visa."

Wen-Lung inserts a key into the almirah and opens the door. He pulls out the trousers he plans to travel in. "Did you sew the money into the hem?"

"I did, all except for seven dollars." After purchasing the tickets there's not much spare change left.

"It's ridiculous how Indian Customs only allows us to take seven dollars abroad. Gabriel said that it won't even get me from the airport to his apartment," he snorts. "Maylei, you're a good woman. I feel awful about leaving you both."

I swallow hard and nod.

Jay-Son's delighted scream distracts me. "Wheee . . . look, Mama."

He slides down a suitcase. Wen-Lung releases a long sigh and distractedly ruffles Jay-Son's hair. Then he inspects the straps and the locks on the luggage. All he needs for his new life abroad are contained in them. I run through a mental checklist of all the things that I have packed: passport, curry powder for Joy, curry powder for Gabriel . . .

• 4 •

Wen-Lung is gone. I'm alone with a toddler and another baby on the way. The nights are long, and during the lonely hours sleep plays hide-and-seek with me. During the days I stay busy at work, and at home Jay-Son keeps me absorbed with his antics. He can't understand why he can't see his papa anymore.

I tell him, "He's gone to Canada."

"Where's Canada?"

"It's a place far away. One day, you and I will take an airplane and fly there too, sweetie." I tilt his chin up, the skin soft and smooth on my fingers. His eyes widen as round as marbles and his lashes fan his cheeks when he blinks. "An airplane? Up there?" His lips tremble, and he bursts into tears. "I want to see my papa now!"

We avert a tantrum, and with two biscuits in his hand, he runs outside to play.

On Sunday Jay-Son and I visit my parents as usual. I'd given up attending Sunday mass at the small local church soon after my wedding, Wen-Lung was not religious, so I gladly lapsed from my Catholic faith. Spending time with my parents and siblings was more appealing than listening to the rigid sermons of our priest. We walk, and I have to carry Jay-Son part of the way. My parents' home is a single-story building facing the main paved road that winds through Tangra, a ten-minute walk from my home. It is where I grew up. Holding Jay-Son tight in my arms, I carefully cross the wooden plank bridging the road to the front door, over an open sewer. Father glances up from the desk where papers and notebooks are strewn everywhere. He teaches history and geography to Classes Five and Six at the local Chinese school. Everyone calls him Hau Lao-Tzu or Teacher Hau.

"Pa, have you eaten breakfast?"

Our Hakka greetings always involve the three main meals.

He takes his reading glasses off and his face breaks into a wide grin. Rising up he opens his arms wide. "Jay-Son, let me look at you. What a big boy you are. Come to Kung-Kung." It's how little kids address grandfathers.

Jay-Son leans forward in my arms, straining to free himself. Kung-Kung always has a treat for him hidden somewhere inside his desk.

I hand him over to Father. While the two chatter on about Jay-Son's adventures and the airplane he will himself fly to Canada one day, I go inside to the middle room. The trundle bed that my elder sister Jinlei and I slept in until we left to get married is still tucked underneath the big bed. Three folded canvas cots lean against the wall, one for each of my younger brothers, Kam-Yen and Fu-Yen, and a spare one that Jinlei and I fought over. Every night the two guys took their cots out to the front room to sleep.

The sound of running water. I make my way to the kitchen next door where Mother is turning off the faucet. She turns and her eyes light up. "Ah, Maylei, you're early."

She carries a red plastic basin, half filled with white flour, to the round dining table in the middle of the room.

"Ma, what are you making?"

"I'm making shiumai. Mrs Kok is giving a big lunch today and she has ordered fifty."

Mother is famous for her dumplings, stuffed with fish paste and minced pork, which my brother Kam sells door to door every weekday evening. Father's wages were never enough to support the household.

"Where is Jay-Son?" she asks, pouring warm water onto the

flour. The bright sunlight streaming in through the window high-
lights the silver streaks in her hair, which is pulled behind, folded,
and pinned up with a large clip. She looks older than her fifty years.
She was nineteen when she married Father and twenty-three when
she gave birth to Jinlei. I wish I could smooth her brow, rid it of its
lines. And yet those lines radiate like sunrays when she smiles.

"Pa is spoiling him as usual. Is Jinlei coming?"

Mother rolls a small piece of dough into a ball between her
palms. "No, she doesn't want to leave her house, because she
thinks she might give birth anytime now."

I pick up a rolling pin and start to flatten the balls into thin
wraps. "I still have another four months," I say, patting my belly.

"Maylei, why did you let Wen-Lung go to Canada at a time like
this? You need him when your baby is born."

It had to come and I know she's right. "Ma, we've talked about
this before. We didn't expect his visa to be granted so soon. He
had to grab this opportunity. Who knows if he'll ever get another
one?"

"I don't like this. You here with your son and a baby on the way,
while your husband is gone so far away . . . not right for a young
couple to live apart like this." She shakes her head, her eyes brown
pools of concern.

"We have to do this for our children. We want them to have a
better life. I hope they won't have to struggle as much as we do."

"We couldn't give you much when you were growing up, but
you were happy, weren't you?"

Of course I was happy, but I always hungered for more. There's
the sewing machine hidden behind some pots, lying idle in a
corner. I used it to make beautiful clothes for Hakka women
and children, and it had been my ticket to the secretarial school,
which we could not afford. Mother was a seamstress for many
years until her eyes gave up. I realize that I will need to borrow
Ma's machine again.

· 5 ·

Mrs Wong, my landlady, sits on a concrete bench beside the tannery's front gate, hugging her crossed knees. Across from her on another bench, Mrs Kok listens, nodding and clucking, swinging her legs above the ground. Seeing me, Mrs Wong reaches into the hidden pocket of her kimono shirt. Her mouth lifts into a curved line of a smile as she hands me an envelope. "Maylei, here's a letter from your sweetheart."

I smile at her humor, and with a glance at the Canadian postage stamps, I reimburse her for the tip that she must have paid the postman, thank her, and continue inside. The two ladies look disappointed at my departure, having hoped that I would read the letter in their presence and drop tidbits for their curiosity. I open my door, drop my bag on the floor, and rip one end of the envelope as I lower myself on a chair. Wen-Lung's scratchy Chinese script is written on two sheets of lined paper.

"My dear Maylei,

"I hope you are in the best of health. It's been two days since I arrived in Toronto. I'm now staying with Gabriel and his friend Marcus. They rent a two-bedroom apartment together in a neighborhood called St James Town. For now I sleep on the couch in the living room. Gabriel says that in a few weeks I should be able to afford a sofa-bed. With three of us splitting the rent, we can all save money more quickly.

"I'm happy to let you know that I have already found a job at the same automotive parts factory where Gabriel works. He heard about the opening and took me to meet the foreman this morning. This guy hired me on the spot and asked if I could start working tomorrow. I'm not sure what I will do exactly, I just know that I will be in the assembly line. For two weeks I will work from eight in the morning until four in the afternoon, and then the next two weeks from four to midnight. They call these swing shifts here. Gabriel says that the pay is good compared to similar work in other factories.

"Toronto is amazingly quiet for a city. It is clean and has many tall buildings. Unlike Calcutta, I hardly see pedestrians walking the roads except in the downtown area and in Chinatown. You would be impressed if you saw the highways here. Cars move at more than 100 kilometers an hour in many lanes. In Calcutta my scooter barely hits 50 kilometers, and only when there is no traffic.

"Speaking of my scooter, are you still planning to keep it? Perhaps you can learn to drive the scooter after the baby is born. You will be able to save time going to work every day if you don't have to catch the bus. As for me here, I have to take a subway train and then transfer to a bus to get to the factory.

"On the day that I arrived, Gabriel and Marcus took me to a restaurant called McDonald's for dinner. I ate my first hamburger there. Remember how you and I tried a hamburger once at Oasis to celebrate our first real date after we got engaged? That meal must have cost me about a day's wage, but Gabriel said that here a hamburger costs less than an hour's pay. We also bought finger chips which they call French fries. I miss your cooking, and it doesn't help that the meat tastes strange and soft."

Wen-Lung inquires about the family, and whether I've seen his parents. Does Jay-Son miss him? And he ends without any endearment or hint of an emotion. Like most Hakka men he believes that showing a tender and vulnerable side is a woman's trait.

I fold the letter and a wave of sadness washes over me, the kind you feel when you think you've lost something but can't quite figure out what. Aloud I say, "Be happy for him. He'll send for us soon." I don't know how he managed to find work without legal papers in Canada. I have heard that one has to have certain pieces of identification to allow you to work there. Somehow Wen-Lung did it, but he doesn't say how. Of course he needs to be mindful about what he writes in case the letter falls into wrong hands. Despite this knowledge I still feel unreasonably disappointed at the lack of passion in his words.

Wen-Lung and I have never shared our innermost thoughts. We have a comfortable and passionless relationship. As with most Tangra marriages, a matchmaker had introduced us. Mother said that love grows between a couple after they have lived together for some time and produced children. Perhaps she is right, after all I do think my mother and father love each other. But I don't know if what I feel for my husband can be described as love. If not love, then what else can it be? So what if my heart doesn't beat a little faster when I see him? If the pain I feel now doesn't compare to the loss I felt saying goodbye to Keith?

Weeks later, another letter from Wen-Lung. He has been paid a few times already, and he now owns a sofa-bed. He has met other Hakka men from Tangra and other parts of Calcutta. They live close to each other, in the same building or within walking distances. This news only confirms for me that the Indian Hakka community is thriving in St James Town, a place that's now come to life in my imagination.

We exchange letters once a month. I keep the ones I receive from him in a drawer, bundled inside a plastic bag, alongside our wedding pictures. They remind me that I have a husband who is working hard to reunite us with him one day.

· 6 ·

Mr Wilson watches me with a thoughtful expression from his desk across the room. "Maylei, when was the last time you took a holiday?"

"Oh, is there a problem? I took a few days off for the Chinese New Year back in February."

"No, no problem. You look tired. When is your baby due?"

"Sometime in October . . . two more months to go. I'm saving my vacation so that I can take a few weeks off when my baby comes. Is that okay with you?"

"Of course, that's fine. I'm not a monster, my dear. How long have you worked for me? Five, six years? You are like my daughter now. And oh, speaking of my daughter, Astrid wants to see you soon."

"Tell Astrid I'd love to meet her for lunch. Ask her if this Friday will work?"

Astrid has remained my friend and confidante despite my breakup with her brother. Even after her marriage to Roger Lobo and with two children, we meet whenever we can. She's like an older sister in more ways than my own sister, whom I love dearly, but I can't tell Jinlei my innermost thoughts the same way that I can tell Astrid.

I met Astrid when she taught a shorthand class at her father's secretarial school. She introduced me to her brother on my nineteenth birthday, having insisted on taking me out for lunch, and inviting Keith to join us at the last minute. Keith was apparently sliding into depression at the break-up with his girlfriend, and Astrid thought that I could help her cheer him up. I saw no traces of suffering when I met Keith, who seemed more interested in finding out about me than in brooding over his failed relationship. Where I had gone to school, what I liked to eat, what movies I enjoyed, did I have a boyfriend. By the end of the meal, he had wrung a promise out of me to meet him again.

◆ ◆ ◆

On Friday around noon I hear Astrid's bracelets jingling in the corridor before I see her plodding in, wearing a bright green and yellow polyester churidar tunic that hangs comfortably over her baggy salwar. Her matching green chunni scarf trails gaily behind her.

"Astrid, you look—" I choke and sputter, and a strange sound escapes from my throat as I see him.

The unmistakable long chin now sporting a half-inch beard, spreading over cheeks more hollow than I remember. Amber brown eyes, hair stylishly unruly and cropped shorter than before. A mature-looking Keith walking paces behind his sister.

When did he come back from Canada? He strides in, his six-foot frame looking trimmer, and his white t-shirt stretching across shoulders much wider than before. When our eyes meet his jaws tense, and a shadow skims across his face.

I rise clumsily and my middle girth bumps the desk in front of me. Astrid flings her arms around my neck, pecks my cheeks, and gushes, "Look at you, pregnant and still slim. How do you manage that? I look like an elephant next to you."

Astrid has been fighting a losing battle with her weight since the birth of her children. I attempt to smile and, embarrassed, let my gaze fall on the protrusion half-way down my body. I can feel his stare scrutinizing me, and I squirm in my already hot skin.

"Hello Keith, when did you come home?" I say, trying to sound cool.

Keith greets me with a stiff smile. I tell myself Astrid will have to deal with my wrath later. Why didn't she call ahead to warn me? Mr Wilson never mentioned his son was home, but why would he? He never knew about Keith and me.

Astrid grimaces and shrugs. "Keith arrived yesterday. We're having a big celebration for my mom's sixtieth birthday next week. I was visiting her, and he decided to come with me just as I was about to leave."

"Sorry to crash your party. I needed to satisfy my curiosity about something." His voice sends an icy tremor down my back, and I wipe the sweat off my brow with my handkerchief.

Astrid waves at her father. "Dad, do you want to join us for lunch?"

Mr Wilson ambles towards us with a wide grin. "No, dear. You go ahead without me."

He looks at his son with a proud gleam in his eyes. "I never thought my son would be bigger than me one day."

Keith chuckles and playfully rubs his father's paunch. "Taller, Dad . . . not bigger." He turns and catches me watching them, and for a fleeting second he continues to smile. I allow myself to smile back tentatively.

I cannot blame him if he never wants to speak to me again. I hope he will forgive me one day. For a moment I wish I could turn the clock back and tell him that I will follow him to the end of the world. I give myself an invisible shake, and the moment passes. I am a married woman with a child, and another one coming, not a schoolgirl.

The three of us stroll over towards a restaurant a small block away. I know that Keith's unhurried pace belies a pent-up energy. I can peek at the blue denim-clad limbs on Astrid's other side. We reach the restaurant where Keith and I first met. If entering here brings back memories, he masks his expression well. He pulls a chair out for me. As I sit down, his palm brushes my arm, my skin tingles, and he goes to sit across from Astrid and me. I watch him rub his bearded chin, a familiar gesture. He is as uncomfortable as I am. When he catches me staring at him I quickly glance down at the menu: chicken and mutton biriyani, seekh kebab, tikka kebab, chapati, paratha, and a list of foods that blur in front of my eyes.

"How is Leona?" I ask casually. The last time Astrid and I met she'd told me that he was dating an Anglo-Indian girl whom he met at a New Year's Eve dance in Toronto. In a perverse way, I want to hear how he's moved on since our break-up.

"Uh, fine, I guess. We broke up last month," he says in a non-committal voice.

My mood lifts and I'm hungry. We order chicken curry, naan and biriyani, and brother and sister banter with each other. Finally, Keith sits back and answers our questions about Canada. He works as a computer programmer, at a large bank, with cowork-ers from many parts of the world. He shares an apartment with his friend Dennis. He describes shopping malls with merchandise I can only dream about. By the time the waiter brings our food, I can already see Keith in his Toronto setting.

During a lull Keith asks, "Maylei, when are you joining your husband in Toronto?"

"I wish I knew. The immigration process takes a long time."

Astrid squeezes my thigh. "How are you coping without Wen-Lung?" She asks, her voice filled with concern.

I fake a nonchalant shrug and blink back the tears. "Okay, I guess."

"Oh dear, let's change the topic." She puts an arm around my shoulders and draws me close.

Keith gives a frown and growls, "What kind of a man leaves his pregnant wife and child this long?"

My face turns red and I pull away from Astrid. "Wen-Lung and I agreed to do this. It wasn't his decision alone," I say sharply.

"Of course, you both decided together, dear," Astrid rubs

my arm soothingly.

Keith mutters, "I'm sorry."

The waiter appears and begins to remove the dishes, the clatter of plates dispelling the uncomfortable silence. The brief intimacy I experienced while Keith drew Astrid and me into his world has vaporized, and all too soon our time together ends.

After our lunch, although my heart cries out for another glimpse of him, thankfully I never see him again. Two weeks later Mr Wilson mentions that Keith has gone back to Canada, and I breathe a sigh of relief. And yet thoughts of him preoccupy me.

Why did he come back? It was clear to me that he still harbored the pain and resentment at my rejection of him. The sight of me carrying another man's child must have gnawed at him.

As for me, I used to wonder what it would be like to meet Keith; now I know. The pain never left.

· 7 ·

Mrs Wong shuffles past the hydraulic press in the tannery and weaves between the two work tables laden with finished leather stacked two feet high. Standing before my wok, I use a spatula to mix beaten eggs into minced pork. She comes and stops in front of me, the clay stove between us, and throws me a simpering smile. "Ah Maylei, good that I found you before you started eating your dinner."

"Mrs Wong, to what do I owe the honor of your visit?" I can't ward off the sense of unease rising from my gut.

She clears her throat. "Mok-Shin and I are wondering if Wen-Lung will be coming back to work for us."

I've been expecting this question. I reply, "Wen-Lung will stay in Canada until his airline ticket expires next month." This has been my stock response to every person who has asked.

She shifts her weight and uses a handkerchief to wipe the sweat on her brow. "We need help in the tannery. Mok-Shin needs to hire someone to take over the work. Don't worry, he's not ending your husband's employment yet."

"Of course, I understand. He should go ahead and do whatever is best." I wait for the noose to tighten some more.

"Well, Mok-Shin has spoken to someone who can start to work for us in two weeks. The new employee will need accommodation here, and he has a family." Her sparse curly hair, unnaturally black against her fair skin, frames an apologetic grimace on her round face.

I lift the wok away from the fire with exaggerated care. "Are you asking me to move out?"

"Oh no, no, goodness me, we're not mean people. We don't want to do that to you and Jay-Son while you're pregnant. We need your room because it's the only one we can assign to an employee living with us." She pauses. "You know that room where we store the finished leather? We can empty that out for you."

I know the space well; it's right behind the hydraulic press. To access it one must walk ten paces past the giant machine, which goes thumping as the workers feed leather into its massive jaws. Wen-Lung spent many hours in that room. He would measure the finished leather, write their measurements with a chalk on the backside of each piece, and tally the numbers on an adding machine later. Then he rolled the leather pieces in brown paper—five to a pack—for the customers to transport away in three-wheeled Tempo vans. The room contains two small windows facing the neighboring tannery's wall across a two-foot alleyway.

I am not moving up in the world, but at least I'm not moving out, and the room she's offered is a little larger than the one I'm in now. I thank Mrs Wong. "When should I get ready to move?"

Mrs Wong's gaze drops to my stomach. "You are going to have this baby in a month or so. Let's get you into your new space as soon as possible. I will get two of the workers to help you next Saturday. Is that okay?"

It could be worse; I could be moving back to my parents' place where my growing family will crowd their already cramped quarters. "Yes, of course. You are too kind."

"One more thing," she drops her voice into a conspiratorial tone, "We've decided to reduce your rent by fifty rupees since the space is dark and noisy."

I make a happy face to show my appreciation. I can certainly use the extra money. In my mind I can already see the stark white-washed walls and the naked yellow bulb along with a white tube light hanging from the ceiling. I brush the image aside and thank Mrs Wong again, already thinking about the unused curtain material that I will use to cheer up the room.

Mrs Wong turns to leave but stops halfway. "I almost forgot another matter. You'll have to share your kitchen with our new employee's wife."

The move brings an unexpected benefit besides the reduced rent. The extra floor space I use for my work as a ladies' tailor. My customers are the trend-setters in Tangra, and word about my return to dressmaking spreads quickly. Within weeks there is more demand than I can cope with.

"Wen-Lung Ta-Sao, this dress is beautiful," Nina says, addressing me as Wen-Lung's wife and elder sister-in-law all in one, in the traditional way. She surveys her reflection in my mirror and she is happy. She gracefully twirls one way and then the other. The breeze from the ceiling fan lifts her skirt higher each time she spins, and the little yellow and red flowers on the fabric chase one another in billowing circles.

From a chair, Lili watches her cousin's performance. She snickers, "Your future husband will swoon when he sees you. It's perfect for your first date this Sunday."

Nina blushes prettily and giggles. "Do you really think so? I want to make a good impression on him. He's come all the way from Austria. My mom says that his matchmaker showed him pictures of many girls, but he was very picky."

Lili sighs enviously. "You're so lucky, Nina. I heard that he owns a restaurant in Vienna. I wish someone from Canada would come and sweep me off my feet. Not that I have anything against Austria."

"Don't worry, your turn will come soon. Truthfully though, I would prefer to go to Canada instead of Austria. Still I'm happy to go abroad and leave Tangra."

I feel envious. A sharp twist in my belly reminds me of my

ballooning girth and my baby, who must be impatient to meet the world.

Lili looks anxiously at me. "Is something wrong? Are you in pain? You're not going to have the baby right now, are you?"

I pat my stomach. "No, I don't think so. The baby isn't due for a few more weeks. Sometimes he plays football in here. Or maybe she's dancing."

Nina says, "Oh, good, will you be able to get my other dress ready next week then? I'll need it for my engagement party."

"Of course I'll have it ready for you."

"What if the baby arrives before you finish it?" she wrinkles her brow. "If only I knew how to sew too, then I can make my own clothes."

"Yeah, me too," Lili says. "Just imagine all the clothes we can have if we could sew."

"Dressmaking isn't too hard to learn," I tell them. "The weird thing is that you think you will make all kinds of new things to wear after you finish learning, but nothing can be further from the truth."

Nina wiggles into her trousers. "That's not going to happen to me." She zips up and gazes into my eyes. "Will you teach me?"

Taken aback by her directness, I tap my chin, pretending to think. "Hmm . . . maybe after my baby is born I'll consider it."

I have to admit that the idea never occurred to me before. But this could be a good opportunity to earn a decent side income. The more I think about the possibility, the more attractive it seems. If I take in five or six girls at a time, I could run a class every Saturday for a few hours. I may even give up sewing for other people.

I look around the room. There's enough floor space to spread out paper patterns and other sewing materials. My old place would have been too small to run a class. I silently thank Mrs Wong for this blessing that came disguised as a dark shabby room.

8

"Ma, wake up." Doubled up in pain beside her bed, I shake her arm. My water broke on my way to the bathroom, and a wetness trickles down my thigh as my contractions get urgent. It's my baby announcing its arrival.

A few days ago Ma had insisted that I stay with her during the final stage of my pregnancy so that she could keep an eye on Jay-Son and me.

Mother struggles to open her eyes. "Uh-uh, what did you say?" Another contraction seizes my body and I cry out. Ma jolts upright. "Maylei, is the baby coming? What time is it?"

"Yes Ma. I should go to the hospital right away. It's a few minutes after two. Wake Fu up."

My brother Fu works as a handyman for Way-Son Lee, owner of the large tannery across the street, who has already offered the use of his car for this occasion.

My father and Mr Lee spend many evenings together after dinner reminiscing about their childhoods in Canton, China. They immigrated to India in their late teens. In Tangra there is an ongoing bitter feud between two dominant groups whose surnames are Lee and Liu, and sometimes Mr Lee gets excited about the latest dispute. Then Father, who's on neither side, calms him down.

"Ma!" I try to yell, but only a whimper comes out. "Ma . . ."

Faint with pain, in the midst of dressing up for the hospital, I hear a child's cries. My gaze falls on Jay-Son sitting up on the bed, but I am too numb to react. Darkness envelops me.

◆ ◆ ◆

I become conscious lying on a bed with a pounding in my head. An overhead yellow bulb glows with a strange incandescent halo. My hands move to my stomach. It feels empty. In panic I try to sit up, open my mouth to speak.

A hand touches mine. "Maylei, are you awake?" The voice sounds distant. It's Mother.

With effort I focus my gaze on her face. "Where's my baby?" I whisper.

Someone says in Hindi, "Don't move. You're still too weak, and you'll bleed to death."

A white form has taken shape behind Mother's chair. She starts to approach me just as someone moans and another person screams in pain. I realize that I am in a hospital ward. The nurse in a white uniform now hovers over me, lifts my hand, and adjusts the tube at my wrist.

"Where's my baby?" I ask again.

"Don't worry about your baby. Go back to sleep," the nurse says.

Against my will, I drift off. I hear Wen-Lung calling out to me. He smiles at me holding Jay-Son in his arms. I ask him to bring our new baby to me. He stares at me with blank incomprehension. "I want to see my baby," I say.

He vanishes. Where he stood before, only Jay-Son remains, crying. "What's the matter?" I ask and reach for him. He continues to cry. I lean forward to reach him, but he remains elusive. No matter what I do, I cannot get near enough to touch him. I scream in frustration.

"Maylei, everything will be all right," Mother says in a soothing tone, her fingers caressing my arm.

"What happened?" I whisper.

I hear the hitch in her voice, thick with emotion. "She was stillborn."

Nothing in my life has prepared me for the anguish I feel—this hollowing of my soul—intangible, yet also physical. My womb feels empty, yet my bosom bursts with life. How is this possible? Surely if I close my eyes and drift off, I will wake up with my precious infant nursing at my breast.

Father says, "Maylei, the nurse wants to know if you want to see your baby."

I nod and follow his gaze toward the far end of the ward near the door. Why does the sun still shine over there? A nurse makes her way through the aisles with a bundle in her arms. She reaches my bed after what seems like an eternity. "Mrs Chen, here she is," she says in a hushed voice as though she doesn't wish to wake my little girl.

My arms ache to hold her, and for a brief moment I believe she's alive. I cradle my baby, letting my tears fall on her peaceful face, reposed like Sleeping Beauty—except she will never wake. I don't understand how it's possible that this perfectly formed babe will never breathe. I take in every detail of her face. Her nose turns up impishly hinting at a mischievous spirit, but I will never find out for sure. Her tiny lips press together in a little pout, perhaps disappointed at being snuffed out before she's even had a chance to test this world. I stroke the fingers that will never curl around mine. What happened?

The nurse leans over the bed to take my baby away. I wrap the swathing blanket tighter around her and draw her closer to me. The nurse clucks like a hen. "Mrs Chen, you must give her back to me."

"Please let me keep her for a few more minutes," I whisper. "Just a few more minutes."

She strides toward another bed to tend to a woman and her live baby fretting in her arms.

Mother gets up from the chair and sits on the bed. Her tears run as fast as mine. She traces her fingers on my little girl's pale cheeks. Father shuffles closer. I can sense his sorrow even though he remains dry-eyed.

All too soon the nurse returns. This time she takes my baby without asking. I want to wail and scream at the Christian God I no longer believe in, and at Mother's Taoist gods, for this injustice, but only a fit of sobbing escapes my lips. I want to expunge the pain, but only manage to hug myself while I let the ache gnaw at my soul without mercy.

Later I wake up to Jay-Son's childish prattling, and briefly, my spirit lifts. But the impact of what has happened crushes me anew, and I want to curl up again and drift off to sleep. But Jay-Son has seen my open eyes.

"Mama, when are you coming home?" he lisps. He squirms down from my mother's lap and rests his hands on my arm. "You sleep too long."

Mother says, "Shh . . . don't disturb your mama. Come back here."

I smile wanly and reach out. "It's okay, let him come to me."

Mother says, "Mr Lee bought a tricycle for Jay-Son yesterday."

"Please thank him for me," I tell her.

A few minutes later Jay-Son tugs at his grandmother's trousers, impatient to return to his new tricycle. I watch their retreating backs with a heavy heart. My only child does not seem to need me; worldly pleasures entice him. My stillborn babe will never need me—she was never meant for this world. Where is my husband right now? Is he thinking about us? I try to visualize a sad-looking Wen-Lung, but I can't. Instead I see Keith and shake the image away.

A doctor comes on his rounds, and I get some answers. He says that my baby suffocated on her way out because the umbilical cord was wrapped around her neck. No one is to be blamed for what happened.

Then why do I feel like I failed my baby? I failed my husband, and I failed my son. I have failed everyone who loves me.

9

Mother insists that Jay-Son and I stay with her while I recover from the devastating childbirth. "If you go home, no one will look after you." After a couple of weeks, despite her protests, I stuff our things into my cotton satchels, ready to go. I have to push myself out of the depression and despair and look after Jay-Son.

"You're not ready yet, Maylei. It's not even a month. You lost a lot of blood and you're still not eating properly."

"Everything will be fine, Ma. I must go home."

To mollify her I agree to all her instructions. A short rickshaw ride later, I find myself back in my own home with mixed feelings—dread at having to face my demons on my own, and relief that Mother is no longer hovering over me.

Jay-Son's absorption with himself prevents me from drowning in self-pity. Oblivious to my loss, he forces me to pay attention to him. He tries to ride his new tricycle in our room, and bumps into the furniture. I drag myself out of my room and let him ride inside the tannery instead. I watch him weave in between the work tables and go back and forth from the front door to the kitchen. He wants to show off his tricycle to his friends and ventures outside against my wishes, then returns crying when he takes a tumble.

My demons come out during the nights in self-recriminations as I lie awake, replaying the events leading up to the stillbirth. What signs did I miss during my pregnancy? Is this retribution for my sin—the sin of loving someone else while being married to another? I toss from side to side, and my mind wanders into a forest of morbid thoughts. I recall how Mrs Lin from two doors down lost her six-year-old son who drowned in a pond in the neighborhood. The crazed look in her eyes—do I have the same tortured look now?

Anyone can claim to empathize with a mother's suffering, but you can never truly understand the depth of the emotional trauma until you have experienced the same loss. I was sorry for Mrs Lin back then, now I breathe her sorrow and live the same never-ending nightmares.

A month after my loss, I return to work at St Agnes's. Gita, the chubby student with the smiling round face is the first one to visit. Lips quivering, she comes to me and squeezes my arms gently. "Welcome back," she says in English in a hushed tone as if loud sounds would rip me apart.

Mrs Gupta, the shorthand teacher is next. "Let me know if you need any help, Maylei." She chokes back tears. Mr Wilson arrives at nine and gazes at me the way Father did when I was discharged from the hospital. He clears his throat and says, "Maylei, my dear, if you need anything, please let me know. Take it easy until you're strong again."

"Thank you, Mr Wilson, you're too kind."

"Astrid will be coming to visit you today. She can't wait to see you."

The stream of well-wishers continues throughout the morning. At noon Astrid strides in and unceremoniously wraps her arms around me, rocking me against her ample bosom like I'm a child. "Maylei, my dear, you must come out for lunch with me."

"Thanks, Astrid. Not today, please, I've brought my lunch."

"Okay, I'll let you off the hook today, but I won't take no for an answer next time."

She keeps returning. Sometimes she brings lunch for her father and me, and sometimes we go downstairs and grab street food—fried potato pancakes in chickpea curry, or round balls of puchka. It seems I haven't lost my appetite for the fried balls stuffed with potatoes and cucumber. I can eat eight of these dipped in tamarind water and still crave for more. Astrid cheers me with her stories about her children. She brings me up-to-date with the latest Bollywood hit movies. She plugs me into juicy gossips about Manju, a mutual friend, who is cheating on her husband.

I plunge myself into the work and before long, except for the hole in my heart, it doesn't feel like I have left at all.

I receive a letter from Wen-Lung filled with remorse for being away at a time like this. What can I say except to plead with him not to punish himself? I wish my mind would follow the same advice. How do I drive my nightly monsters away? The entire universe is conspiring to make me feel better, yet in a perverse way, I want to hold on to my sorrow as if anything less would betray my dead baby. Pao-Chin, my friendly but nosey neighbor who often walks with me to the market square, becomes my guardian, feeding Jay-Son and me whenever Mother's food runs out. Like a finely tuned antenna, she knows exactly when to knock on my door with a bowl of noodles or rice and a stir-fried something.

Finally the illusion of time standing still comes to an end. December blends into January, and with the Chinese New Year just weeks away, I am reminded that many months have passed since Wen-Lung left. Not in any mood to celebrate, I still begin to prepare for the occasion. But with each passing day my resentment towards Wen-Lung—a tiny spark initially—begins to grow. I know it's irrational, because we agreed we wanted to go to Canada, and this was the only way open.

One afternoon, a few days before the end of the lunar calendar year, I park my scooter in the tannery after a long day at the office. As I begin to head for my room, eager to set eyes on Jay-Son, Mrs Wong waves an envelope at me. "Ah, Maylei, you always look so sad. Maybe this will cheer you up. Here's a letter from Canada. Perhaps Wen-Lung will come home where he belongs, huh."

"Thank you, Mrs Wong."

Inside my room, I scan the two pages Wen-Lung has written. With trembling fingers I read it again. This is the first piece of good news in a long time. Wen-Lung has applied for permanent residency in Canada, and he says he has a fair chance of success. The process will cost money, of course. Wen-Lung is prepared for this; he has saved a good part of his pay since he started work.

A noise at the door, and Jay-Son rushes in, Didi right behind him. "Mama, look what I made." He thrusts a paper boat into my hand. "Do you like it?"

Putting on an earnest expression I examine the lined paper—a page from a child's notebook—folded to look like a boat with lop-sided ends. I give a smile and lift Jay-Son up. "Oh, baby, you are so clever."

Jay-Son points at Wen-Lung's letter on the desk. "Can I make another boat with that?"

"Oh no, that's a letter from Papa."

He turns to stare into my eyes, his fingers touching my chin. "Where's Papa?"

"He's in Canada, remember? We'll join him soon," I tell him confidently.

He writhes in my arm, inpatient to get away and play. His papa is an old memory, no longer relevant to his world of games and tricycle races with the neighborhood kids. I watch him scoot out the door, carefree and full of life. Didi hurries after him. I change out of my work clothes and head for the kitchen.

Surprisingly, for the first time in weeks, I catch myself humming a tune from a Hindi movie. Maybe I'll take up Pao-Chin's offer to watch a new hot Bollywood release with her on Sunday.

· 10 ·

Astrid squeezes my hands across the table, her golden bangles making a clink as they touch the marble surface. She rattles off a few dishes from the menu to the waiter standing at the entrance to our booth. After he leaves, she frowns at me. "Spill it out, Maylei. What's going on? I can see it in your face, so don't try to deny it."

I look into her eyes, as concern ripples over her face. Dragging out a long breath I tell her, "I'm tired of waiting to go to Canada. Wen-Lung's application for landed status was rejected. I asked him to come home, but he says he hasn't given up."

"Oh dear, I'm so sorry to hear that. How is he able to still stay in Canada?"

"He's hired an immigration lawyer who is handling his case. Somehow he's been granted a temporary permit to stay while the lawyer files an appeal or something. He tells me not to worry, but he doesn't understand that I just want him back here."

She knits her eyebrows together until they almost meet. "What kind of a marriage is this? You've been living apart for over two years, and the end is not yet in sight. Why don't you divorce him?" She just stops short of mentioning her brother Keith.

I sniff into my handkerchief before answering. "Please don't say that, Astrid. You know I will never divorce my husband unless he does something really bad. You know I've put Keith behind me. He should do the same and move on."

"I'm sorry, I shouldn't say these things even if they're true. It's hard for me to see you struggle and look so sad all the time. You deserve some happiness. Your husband should realize that you need him with you now."

"The plan to go to Canada was something we agreed upon together, so it's not all his fault."

But lately I've been wondering whether we are paying too high a price for an elusive dream. Of course, had I married Keith, not only would I be with the man I love, I would also be in Toronto by now. But such thoughts make me feel unclean, like I'm cheating on my husband. And how do I know what Keith would be like as a husband? Is there a guarantee in a marriage?

"Well," Astrid purses her lips. "I'm here for you if you need me for anything."

"Thanks, Astrid. If it weren't for you, I couldn't have made it through my worst moments." I realize that her presence as she talked and listened to me during those bleak days got me through more than my mother and sister did. They didn't understand that in order to get past my loss, I needed to talk about it. To avoid causing me pain, they danced around the topic of my baby's death, but Astrid let me pour my soul out.

"Maylei, I only did what a good friend would do under those circumstances. Now I wish you would ask yourself what you really want. You're young, beautiful and still a great catch for any man. But you've got this queer notion about your parents' reputation and not wanting to do anything to make them look bad. When will you start to live for yourself and ask what makes Maylei happy?"

I shake my head. "I'm Chinese and bound by duty to respect my parents and elders. And I live in Tangra."

"Are you suggesting that I'm disrespectful?"

"Sorry, I didn't mean that. You are a wonderful daughter, and your dad is very proud of you. I've heard him say so myself."

"Well, Dad's side of the family has always been liberal. When he married a Chinese, they welcomed her. Anglo-Indians know what it feels like to come from two different cultures and belong to neither."

Astrid doesn't understand what it's like to be Hakka and living in Tangra. I recall how when I was a teenager I was caught once meeting a boy secretly at a movie theatre, and the long lecture I received on the virtues of keeping a pure reputation. I steal a glance at Astrid, so obviously different. I reach across the table to touch her hand. "Thank you for being my friend."

The waiter appears with our food, ending my brief introspection.

◆ ◆ ◆

Mother also takes her turn at reminding me about my absent husband. "What is the news from Wen-Lung these days?" she says, scrubbing Father's shirt collar with a wooden brush, as we crouch before two aluminum washing basins on the kitchen floor.

I tell her, "Ma, the immigration process takes a long time. Wen-Lung says that he's suffered a minor setback. His lawyer is filing papers for him again." I don't mention that this news is a couple of months old, and I haven't received word from him since then.

"I don't like this. Young couples shouldn't stay apart for so long. He has needs . . . you have needs . . . " Her voice trails off in embarrassing silence.

Red-faced, I say, "Ma, don't worry about us." But what Mother calls "my needs" have caused me a few restless nights recently. In the dark sometimes I reach over to my husband's side of the bed only to find it empty. Sleep catches up with me only after I toss and turn many times, my yearnings remaining unsatisfied.

She passes Father's shirt to me to rinse and pulls a pair of dirty trousers from the basin. "Your mother-in-law complained to me the other day that someone saw you with an Indian man at Flury's." She lets her own concern hang between us, like a question mark.

"It was a harmless afternoon tea break, Ma, with my boss and his daughter. Astrid was in the toilet when Wen-Lung's uncle saw us. He glared at us and left without making any attempt to talk to me. My mother-in-law should pay more attention to her own daughter's illicit affairs instead of listening to gossip about me."

"Shush, don't be saying nasty things. How was your uncle supposed to know that your girlfriend was there too, if he couldn't see her?" She pauses, before letting out, "And what about the rumor that Wen-Lung is seeing another woman?"

My chest tightens. I fake nonchalance, quirk an eyebrow and say in an even tone, "What about it? It's not true. I think that people love to gossip."

"How do you know it's not true? Have you asked him about it?"

"Ma, if Pa were cheating on you, would he tell you?"

"What kind of nonsense is that?" she mutters and glares at me.

If the circumstances were different, I would have laughed at her response. The rumors bother me more than I will let her know. It's hard to separate truth from gossip when Wen-Lung's letters are long on everyday activities and short on details of things that matter. His obsession, bordering on paranoia, with keeping his immigration process out of his letters as much as possible, only fuels the gossip. I have nothing to fend off the rumors.

Mother gets up with a groan, straightens her back, shuffles towards the bathroom and closes the door behind her. While my hands dip a shirt in and out of the water in the basin mechanically, my mind wanders into the past, to the events leading up to my marriage to Wen-Lung.

My parents found out about Keith because someone in Tangra saw us together. Mother pleaded with me to stop seeing him. Father reasoned with me that the community would question his credibility as a teacher if he couldn't even discipline his own daughter. It was bad enough that Keith's father was Anglo-Indian, but having a Chinese mother made him even more mixed, and so much less suitable for me.

I cried and pleaded but Mother insisted that she would hire the matchmaker Mrs Lam to find me a husband in Tangra. Within a week, Mrs Lam came back and told Mother that she would chaperone Wen-Lung and me to a movie. After the film was over, the matchmaker suggested that we go for dinner to a Chinese restaurant. Knowing there was no hope for Keith and me, I nodded my agreement. Wen-Lung didn't seem to need any persuasion and looked relieved when I agreed to continue our evening, a sign that I'd agreed to marry him. We were engaged within weeks and our wedding followed seven months later.

I gave up love for the promises of honor and respect. Now I hear that my husband is cheating on me. There must be a reason why he hasn't written to me for so long. I try to dismiss another rumor, that he had been spotted with a *fanpoh*, a white woman. Ma's sources even came up with the detail that Wen-Lung had been seen holding the fanpoh's hand.

Wen-Lung in his last letter wrote that I should not believe everything I hear about him. Was this a sign of his guilt?

◆ ◆ ◆

I write to Wen-Lung, hoping to be reassured. But before I get his response, Mother comes to visit one Sunday afternoon and says, "Chen-Poh came by yesterday. She wants to know if Wen-Lung has written to you recently. She's worried."

My mother-in-law worrying about her son's behavior . . . how refreshing! Although I want to lie about my own misgivings, I confess, "I'm worried too, Ma. I haven't heard from him in more than two months."

"There's talk that he got married to a fanpoh. A white woman . . . can you believe his audacity? How can he do that to you and his family? If I'd known he was such a wicked man, I would never have allowed you to marry him."

My heart sinks. I don't even own a legal certificate to prove that Wen-Lung and I are husband and wife. Like many couples in Tangra, my only proof is a clipping from one of the two local Chinese newspapers announcing our wedding. So much for tradition and culture. As far as the rest of the world is concerned, Wen-Lung and I lived together in sin. I want to laugh at the irony, but for the pain that I feel.

· 11 ·

Another Chinese New Year approaches—the third without my husband. The third one that I have to prepare to greet all on my own again. The endless cleaning before New Year's Eve—Wen-Lung would have helped me reach into every corner and crevice of our room while I wiped down the kitchen cupboards and washed every unused utensil—Calcutta is a dust magnet. I sew new clothes for Jay-Son and myself, make deep-fried flour dough and glutinous rice treats with shrimp chips. Traditions to be observed to start the New Year with every auspicious omen.

Another group of girls in my dress-making course, and I look forward to Saturday afternoons with them. They are all in their late teens. I listen to them chat while they draw and cut paper patterns or take turns sewing on the machine that I've borrowed from Mother. One Saturday, Shirley Wu, nonstop talker, looks at me, her scissors suspended midair. "I heard that Chiu Yun-Chi is looking for a wife. He's here visiting his parents. Isn't he your husband's friend?"

My heart lurches. Gabriel in Tangra? The last time I heard from Wen-Lung—over two months ago—he implied that he still shared an apartment with Gabriel. I keep a straight face.

"When did he arrive?"

"Yesterday. One of his younger sisters is my good friend," Shirley purrs, like a satisfied kitten. She has not kept it secret that she desires to marry an eligible bachelor from Canada or the United States.

Betty Liu stops pedaling on the sewing machine and says, "I've heard that as many as thirty to forty ex-Tangra residents will arrive for the big New Year celebrations next week."

Sandra Chung looks up from her paper pattern, one hand pressing a twelve-inch ruler and the other balancing a pencil between two fingers. "Oh, more than that if you believe Mrs Chiu, our biggest gossip."

The girls banter back and forth about the visitors. Now that more and more Hakka from our community live abroad, they come back in droves to celebrate our biggest and grandest festival, when many of them will pick out their future wives. 'Tis the season for engagements and weddings.

The door opens and the maid Didi pokes her head in. She says in Hindi, "There's a *burra sahib* outside waiting to see you."

I frown. Who could he be? I excuse myself from the class and step outside. A familiar figure is pacing the floor beyond the hydraulic press. In his long-sleeved blue and white plaids tucked inside indigo denims, he could be Wen-Lung, except that's not possible. When he turns and sees me, he opens his arms, a white plastic bag dangling from one hand.

"Gabriel!"

He strides towards me with a toothy grin. I attempt to return a smile, but there's only one thought swirling in my head: Wen-Lung has sent him. Questions clamor in my mind, and I hold back the urge to volley them at him right away. We stand awkwardly a few feet apart and I ask, "Have you eaten lunch?"

"Yes, yes. You look well. I bring news from Wen-Lung. Where can we talk?"

I see Mrs Wong watching us by her dining table outside her room. Li-An, the tannery's new manager's wife, stares with unabashed curiosity as she lifts a pot from the stove, taking her time to set it on the kitchen floor. There's no place anywhere out here for a private conversation. I glance at my wristwatch. In fifteen minutes I should be wrapping up the class. "Wait here," I tell him and go inside my room.

"Girls, do you mind if we end the class now? Take your paper patterns and finish cutting them at home if you haven't done so already. Anyone who needs extra help can come early next Saturday."

One by one they gather up their work and troop outside. Shirley, the last one to leave, flashes a coy smile at Gabriel. He responds with a grin and pats his hair in a self-conscious gesture.

I invite him to come inside. He hands me the plastic bag. "Wen-Lung sent some dried goods and candies from Toronto."

"Thanks." I grip the bag by the handles. "Can I offer you some tea?"

He nods and takes a chair. I hold the door ajar and call out to Didi to bring tea. As soon as I turn around, Gabriel blurts out, "Wen-Lung has been desperate to get word to you. He can't write about what he's doing for fear of being found out."

"Found out about what? Is he in trouble?"

"Oh no, it's nothing like that. In order to get landed status, he . . . er . . . uh married a Canadian woman. He had to do that quickly to avoid being deported."

If something bad indeed had happened to Wen-Lung, I think I would handle the news better than hearing this bombshell of a confirmation that the rumors are real. A numbness grips my brain. I lower myself down on a chair. "How can he do this? Does Wen-Lung want to stay in Canada so much that he has given up on our marriage?" My voice quivers despite my attempt to stay calm.

"Oh, no!" Gabriel leans forward, reaches for my hand, but withdraws before he touches me. A flush creeps up to his cheeks. "You misunderstand me. It's a fake marriage. The woman knows, but she's willing to pretend. Once he gets his papers, he will divorce her and pay her an agreed amount."

My breath comes out in short gasps, rage burns in my chest. "Is marriage so cheap in Canada?"

"Please don't—"

"Where is he living these days?"

"Maylei, please don't be angry. This is the only sure way for him to become a landed immigrant. The two of you were never married according to Canadian law. You must have a marriage certificate."

"So, all these years that we've been married means nothing to him."

"Oh, he is still committed to you." Then he shrugs with a resigned look on his face. "I don't want to make light of your marriage to Wen-Lung, but it's not valid in Canada."

"So his fake marriage is more real than our vows. We stood in front of our ancestors and all the gods who cared to listen."

"I don't want you to be upset. Believe me when I say that Wen-Lung is doing all this for you and Jay-Son."

I laugh hysterically. "I'm sorry if I don't sound thrilled. So what do I do now?"

"Wen-Lung says that when he's ready he'll let you know how to proceed. In the meantime, you mustn't speak to anyone about this. No one must find out or it could ruin his chance to stay in Canada."

"I can't keep a lid on this. Rumors are rampant already." I take in a deep breath. "Is he . . . uh . . . does he live with his new wife?"

Gabriel's face clouds and he casts his eyes down. "They have to keep up appearances. The immigration officials poke around to check sometimes, so the marriage has to look real."

"So he's living with her."

"Uh, yes."

"And she's white, of course."

Gabriel nods and I sense that he wishes to be anywhere but here right now. A sound at the door breaks the tension. Didi carries in a tray with two bowls of steaming milk tea and sets them down on my desk. I urge Gabriel to pick up a bowl. He stays a little longer, and we chat vaguely about Tangra and Toronto, then he leaves.

How could my marriage not be real when the entire community witnessed our wedding? Wen-Lung and I had lived together as husband and wife. Surely that must mean something in Canada. But without legal papers, I would be no better than a concubine, a kept woman in Canada. Should Wen-Lung wish to stay with his new wife for the rest of his life, I can do nothing to stop him. Why should he take the trouble to send for us now? And if he did send for us, are we supposed to marry again? And can I turn him down this time?

◆ ◆ ◆

The Year of the Monkey announces its arrival with firecrackers loud enough to scare all the lions and dragons they're meant to welcome. After midnight Jay-Son and I wake up to the clanging of cymbals and steady drumbeats. Holding hands we step out of our room to watch the first of the lions make its way into Mok-Shin's tannery. Drumbeats sound distantly in other parts of Tangra. A teenage boy prances around as he hoists a colorful lion's head of clay. Another boy behind him keeps pace while he holds the streaming tail and ripples the cloth to make golden waves. Mok-Shin lights firecrackers from a candle on the table that Mrs Wong has laden with offerings for the gods. He throws the packet on the floor. As it begins to crackle, the lion's head swoops and dives around the bursting crackers. Jay-Son's hand tightens around mine, but he yells, "Mama, see how the lion jumps. He's not afraid, and neither am I."

I hide a smile as he wraps his arms around my legs when the lion creeps toward us on his way to the alter table where he bows three times. Mok-Shin hands a red envelope of money, *hung pao*, to the leader of the group and then they leave.

In a few short weeks, the festivities become distant memories, and life returns to normal. As normal as it can be for me. Although the sages have advised the young to forgive one another before the end of the year, and to start the new one with a clear conscience, the reality is that the Chinese New Year neither erases existing sins nor wipes out memories of them. The prancing dragons and lions have retired to their lairs along with the drums and cymbals that kept us up all night, scaring the evil spirits away. Children's pockets no longer jingle with coins like they did when they were filled with *hung pao,* the lucky money they received in red envelopes. The street vendors who benefited from the demand for snacks now return to cajoling customers to savor their aloo dum, masala chat, and puchka.

Along with the bright lights and red lanterns have disappeared Gabriel and the other Hakka who congregated in Tangra from Canada, America, Austria, Sweden, and England. Shirley, now engaged to Gabriel, flashes her gold ring around, and the girls admire the engraved Chinese characters representing his given name. While she chatters nonstop about her immigration application, I wonder how much Gabriel has told her about Wen-Lung's marriage.

Now that Wen-Lung's marriage is public knowledge much pity gets directed at me. I cannot reveal to my family that his marriage is fake, fearing that any knowledge of this will jeopardize his stay in Canada. Even so, the truth is difficult to defend and it is easier to let them condemn his action. I keep my silence and play the wronged wife.

My friend, Joy Liang, who lives in the same building as Gabriel in Toronto, writes to me every few weeks. Withholding nothing, she tells me to divorce Wen-Lung, "the bastard." She saw him toss his head back and laugh out loud with his new wife followed by a hug in a public place. He never even held my hand except to slide the engagement ring into my finger. My sister Jinlei advises me to move on and marry someone else. With baby number four in her arms, she lowers her bottom down on my parents' four-poster bed. "That no-good husband of yours doesn't deserve you. Let me set you up with my neighbor's son. His wife died last year and the poor guy seems lonely."

"Leave me alone. I'm not looking for another man, and I'm still married to Wen-Lung."

"Yeah, tell that to him. Apparently you're the only person who believes that. Even Pa and Ma want you to divorce him. All you have to do is place an announcement in the Chinese newspaper."

"That's what got me into this mess in the first place," I mutter. "It seems we put a lot of misguided trust in our newspapers."

Jinlei arches her eyebrows. "What's that got to do with Wen-Lung's behavior?"

"Well, we're not married legally. Where are the documents to prove it?"

"This is ridiculous," she snorts. "Is that the excuse Wen-Lung is using for what he's doing? Then all the more reason to dump him."

"Please don't judge him without all the facts."

"What facts? He's married to a white woman. Isn't that a fact? You're still young, and you need someone to take care of you and Jay-Son."

Silently I curse Wen-Lung and wish I'd listened to Keith and ignored everyone else. But a niggling voice in my head says, "Maylei, you're a coward. You'll never buck tradition."

It's been almost five years since Wen-Lung left us, and more than a year since he divorced his white Canadian wife. And now I am officially engaged to be married to my own husband. Not a day passes that I don't ask myself if I should play the wronged wife instead of the soon-to-be-wed fiancée. But to deny my engagement is to deny my entrance ticket to Canada. And yet I cannot allay the doubts that fill me every time I think about reuniting with my husband. Has he changed? Have I changed? I married Wen-Lung believing that love would grow eventually, but five years is a long time to be apart when we've been married for seven. If it were all about me, I would rather not emigrate, but I know that Jay-Son will surely benefit from the opportunities that I could never give him here in India. Good schools and university education to lift him out of the Calcutta tannery trap.

When I receive the letter from the High Commission of Canada directing me to go to the New Delhi office for an interview, I prepare for the trip with nervous energy. I have travelled out of Calcutta only once before, when I was fourteen, when my parents and I visited a relative in Kharagpur. The journey took two hours but seemed forever, in a slow train so packed with people there was no room to move.

For this journey to Delhi I will be travelling by myself overnight with a berth to sleep on in a lady's compartment, purchased by my brother Fu on the black market.

At five PM I get into a taxi, the neighbors and workers all

having come out to watch me and wish me good luck. Jay-Son is at his grandparents'. Half an hour later, I catch a hazy glimpse of the mighty towers of the Howrah Bridge. Even though I have lived in Calcutta all my life, my breath catches. The bridge lives in our consciousness, spanning over the Hooghly, a tributary of the Ganges, and I have seen it only once before. Tangra is almost like another city, and we Chinese live exclusive lives. As we get closer, the taxi comes to a stop behind a hand-pulled rickshaw. The driver pounds the horn and hurls insults out the window, adding to the colorful expletives around us hardly suitable for a woman's ears, and the cacophony of horns and vehicle noises. Nothing budges except for a few bicycles and motor scooters that weave in and out. Finally we start to inch forward, and it takes more than a good part of an hour to cross to the other side. On the way I strain my neck to catch a glimpse of the Hooghly, and see an assortment of evening bathers and people washing their clothes. In the steel jungle crisscrossing overhead, the lights turn on.

The chaos continues on the other side of the river, where thankfully the taxi pulls up to a curb in front of a massive red building. This is Howrah Station. While I pay the driver, red shirted coolies are already grabbing at the door eager to unload my luggage. I hang on to my overnight bag and wave the porters away, telling them I am all right, there is not much to carry.

Inside the great hall of the station, all is in a flurry, people scurrying after coolies carrying steel trunks—one or maybe two at a time—balanced on their heads. I ask around and a man kindly tells me where to go to take my train.

When the Kalka Mail enters the station, I push my way among the crowd that surges forward toward our compartment door. Someone pinches my buttock. I turn and glare at a young man who glances away nonchalantly and elbows past me. Why am I putting myself through this?

My compartment has four berths. I push my overnight bag to

one of the top ones that will be mine for the night. Three women are sitting on the lower berths, which serve as seats for now, two on one side and one opposite. I say "Namaste," and sit down. They ignore me, I am the foreigner.

The train lurches forward. Men jog alongside on the platform, saying goodbyes, giving instructions to their wives. The young woman with us, sitting by the window, responds to her husband who is carrying a child. Soon he lags behind and stops. The young woman has tears in her eyes as she sits down. Shortly she stands up and slides the compartment door shut, and there is some peace.

The older of the three women, all obviously from one family, opens a two-tier tiffin containing roti, two dry vegetarian curries, and pickles. Soon the three are tearing pieces of roti and scooping out the food. My mouth waters and I bring out my home-made barbeque-pork sandwich which I wash down with masala chai in a clay cup purchased from a passing vendor. As soon as we finish, I clamber up into my berth and try to sleep. The roll and clack of the train is lulling, and just before I fall asleep, all kinds of thoughts go through my head. Luckily, I wake up at dawn; not many people are about and I make my way to the toilet. I know that later it will become unusable.

The train rolls to a stop at Allahabad. I flag down a chai vendor passing by our window. The three ladies also join me in ordering tea. I pull out a roll of Marie biscuits and munch on a few which pass as breakfast. When the train jolts into motion I reach into the front zipper of my overnight bag and pull out a novel.

"You're reading *Jaws*?" someone says in English.

I glance up at the speaker. The woman who had bade a teary-eyed farewell to her husband and son yesterday grins at me. "Uh . . . uh, yes," I say. "Did you read the book already?"

Her eyebrows arch delicately as she gushes, "No, I rarely have time to read these days, but I heard that it's really exciting. Maybe

I'll buy the book in Simla and read it on my way back to Calcutta. The movie was amazing!"

Her sister joins us. Their attitude toward me seems to have thawed. They tell me they'll take the train all the way to the end at Kalka en route to Simla, to attend a wedding. They will stay three weeks there. I don't envy them their extra night on the train.

Our conversations become sporadic, interspersed with reading—they are more interested in their *Filmfare* and *Stardust* magazines and they ooh and aah over the latest Bollywood fashions and heroes. Their mother watches quietly with an indulgent smile, speaking to me occasionally in Hindi.

It is night time when we arrive in Delhi. As we slow down I untie my ponytail, run my fingers through my hair—soot-dusted by now—before retying it again. Not much I can do about my travel-stained appearance. There is a mad scramble to leave, and so I wait for it to subside before I come out. I make my way to the platform, which to my surprise looks exactly like the one I departed from Howrah. At the main hall I look around, wondering who will be here to meet me. My uncle Kin Yee Hau, Father's cousin who visits us sometimes usually during the Chinese New Year, had written to Father that he would send someone to pick me up.

"Maylei Jie Jie!"

Someone is addressing me as elder sister. I turn and see a Chinese young man in his mid-twenties grinning broadly at me. "You are Maylie Jie, aren't you?" he says in Hakka.

"Oh, hello. You must be Joseph, Uncle Kin Yee's son. I barely recognize you. You were only six or seven the last time we met," I say with a huge sense of relief to be rescued me from the mad tumult around me.

"Let me take your bag for you." Joseph relieves me of my overnight bag.

Outside, among a jumble of cars, amidst a din of horns blaring, a red Maruti van is waiting for us. We drive through Delhi in the dark and arrive half an hour later at Lee Kim Restaurant on the south side of Delhi off Sri Aurobindo Marg. Joseph takes me inside through a back door where we enter the kitchen and I meet his mother Auntie Ailee and three younger sisters. One of the girls shows me upstairs to a room with a large four-poster bed and a trundle bed tucked underneath. Uncle Kin Yee comes in a few minutes later. He says, "Maylei, you are looking more and more like your mother as you get older. How is she doing? Such a hard-working woman. And your father? I must visit again soon. Maybe I'll spend the next Chinese New Year with your folks. Make sure you tell your father, huh."

I smile, nod, and answer his questions.

Then he says, "We have closed the restaurant for the day, but you must be hungry. Ailee, go get something for Maylei to eat."

Despite my growling stomach I protest that I'm not hungry; it is the Hakka way. But Auntie Ailee wisely says from the door-way, "Nonsense, you have been traveling a long time. You must eat something."

Gratefully I accept. Uncle Kin Yee shows me around the apartment which occupies the entire upper floor above the restaurant. It looks and feels luxurious compared to my one-room abode and my shared kitchen and bathroom back in Calcutta. I share the three girls' bedroom.

◆ ◆ ◆

The next morning I take a taxi to the High Commission of Canada in the lush green embassy area of the city. Unlike other parts of Delhi, the traffic moves smoothly here. Past the gate, I am directed to a section that looks after visas. It all looks intimidating, and again I wonder if this is all worth it. Why not divorce Wen-Lung and find a local husband? I can send Jay-Son to a good private school. There are already some ten people waiting, all looking jittery and perhaps with the same doubts as mine. When my name is called, I take a deep breath, walk through a door into a corridor, and enter an open door to face the unknown interviewer and an even greater unknown future.

A middle-aged, rather plain-looking woman greets me with the hint of a smile. I stare—transfixed—at the white skin on her face lightly brushed with rouge on the cheeks. Then the red-lipsticked mouth opens and says, "You must be Maylei Hau."

I shake off the stupor that has engulfed me and nod. She introduces herself—I have forgotten her name—and asks me some simple questions about my life: what I do for a living, describe my job, why I want to immigrate to Canada, do I know where Canada is and the name of its capital city. The answers come out of my mouth without hesitation, as most of them are familiar parts of my life, and those that aren't are part of the general knowledge I have acquired over time. In about fifteen minutes or more the interview is over. The woman reaches into a drawer, pulls out an envelope and hands it to me. She stands, smiles and says, "Go home and start packing."

· 13 ·

Lovemaking is a necessary chore and leaves me empty inside. I remember a time when it used to infuse a lingering glow while sleep gently stole my consciousness. Now I listen to Wen-Lung's sputtering snores fragmenting my thoughts. I had put Keith behind me, and with Wen-Lung I had expected an explosive fusion of our bodies and souls, despite the fact that he had gotten married. As I arched toward Wen-Lung, I wanted him to feel the painful emotions I'd buried deep inside. I wanted him to feel the sorrow that I had experienced after the loss of our child. I wanted him to feel my longing for the companionship denied me by his absence, the struggle of my life as a single parent, the lonely nights, and other emotions I can't name.

On this my first night in Toronto, the darkness envelops me like an unfamiliar cloak, suffocating me in its strangeness. My earlier excitement at seeing Wen-Lung again, coupled with the new sights and sounds, has dissipated, replaced by doubts. Jay-Son and I landed at the airport earlier this afternoon where he picked us up in Gabriel's car.

"Look how big you've grown." Wen-Lung put his hands on Jay-Son's shoulders. Jay-Son twisted away, gripping my hand with a sweaty palm.

A shadow crossed Wen-Lung's face. "Give him time," I told him, and admonished Jay-Son to behave towards his father.

Wen-Lung flashed a lopsided grin at me. "It's alright, Maylei, I have waited a long time for this." An awkward silence followed. I wanted to hug him, but we both hung back, embarrassed. Married for seven years, we have lived together for only two of them. An invisible wall stood between us as we stared at each other, hoping to reconnect with what we had before he came to Canada.

"You look good," I said. Indeed, his hair, waved with the bottom tips curled against the collar of his bright red and black button-down shirt, looked different. He used to slick it with oil, puffing it above his forehead.

"Oh, you're not too shabby yourself."

Self-consciously he touched his hair and then rubbed his narrow chin. "Mrs Liu cut and permed my hair last week. It's too expensive to go to the hair salon here."

We followed him into the parking garage. I noticed for the first time that he slouched his shoulders when he walked. As we stood at the elevator lobby with our luggage cart, a middle-aged couple approached us, asking for directions to the departure level. Wen-Lung gave them directions without hesitation. The old Wen-Lung would have looked to me to respond, too embarrassed to speak in English.

He is comfortable in these surroundings, and now I am the awkward one, every uncertain step branding me as a newcomer. When the immigration officer interviewed me at the airport, I sounded stilted. My words would not flow normally, I found his accent hard to understand, and I kept asking him to repeat what he said.

Wen-Lung seems different, and yet he is still the same man I married. What if he finds my ways alien and unattractive? Can we pick up from where we left off as if nothing happened? Can I brush off his fake marriage and pretend it never happened? Was it really fake? It lasted almost two years.

I toss and turn in the double bed. Wide awake from jet lag and super charged with emotions, I slip into Jay-Son's room to check on him. Earlier this evening his initial excitement at having his own room became somewhat muted when I tucked him in. Never having slept by himself before, his trembling lips gave him away when I turned to leave. In a small voice he said, "Mom, can you stay with me until I fall asleep?" I slid in beside him and drifted off along with him. A short while later, Wen-Lung woke me up. Groggy and tired, I crept away to join my husband.

That was more than an hour ago. Now I gaze at my son, the light from the bathroom next door illuminating his face, relaxed in sleep, and all signs of his earlier distress erased. What does the future hold for him and for me? I sigh, turn and tread lightly to the living room, where I lie down on the sofa.

In the semidarkness, I glance around at the unfamiliar silhouettes of our furniture. We have rented a two-bedroom apartment on the tenth floor of an apartment building in a Toronto neighborhood called St James Town. The living room has a sofa and a chair as green as the grass downstairs and feels velvety smooth, only slightly worn in places where the previous owner must have sat frequently. A rectangular coffee table stands between me and a television set that resembles a massive wooden chest without drawers. Behind the sofa, four tan vinyl-covered chairs surround a glossy dining table whose veneer shines with light and dark brown patterns.

Wen-Lung must have spent a small fortune for this gently used assortment. He told me that Shirley, my one-time student and now Gabriel's wife of six months, helped him pick out all the pieces. Compared to our one-room home in Tangra, this apartment looks extravagantly luxurious.

Thinking about the home I've left behind saddens me. Tears well up in my eyes. I grab a tissue from a box on the coffee table and wipe them away—even using a tissue instead of my handkerchief feels strange. My family and friends anchored me in Tangra. Toronto is now our new home. Our lives will be different. Will it be different in a good or a bad way?

A siren wails in the distance. I listen to the traffic on the streets below. No longer do I hear the sounds of dogs barking, or the occasional conversation of people passing by my window, or the night watchman's tuneless whistle as he makes his rounds in the tannery. Two worlds apart, on opposite sides of the globe. Same people in a new environment, and they seem like strangers.

Some of Wen-Lung's friends came to visit earlier this evening. I was still wearing my travel-stained clothes when Michael and Richard knocked on our door, followed by Gabriel and Shirley. They all live in the same building—this is our Tangra in Toronto. Shirley brought dinner, saying, "I made chicken curry and rice . . . not that you haven't eaten Indian food recently." She grinned and glanced at the men. "These guys can't get enough curry. They want it every time we get together."

With half a year's advantage over me, Shirley speaks like she knows about all things Canadian. "You must come with us to Niagara Falls soon." She placed the pot of curry on the stove, picked up a ladle and stirred. "I'm sure Wen-Lung will take you to the grocery store tomorrow. Maylei, you've never seen anything like it before. And the department stores . . . you can try on as many clothes as you want, and you'll never have to sew again if you don't want to." Turning away from me she called out, "Hey, Wen-Lung, A&P has toilet paper on sale. You should take Maylei there and stock up."

I listened to the conversation going on around me, and I couldn't relate. These were my neighbors and friends in our past lives. Nothing and everything has changed.

I stare at the pale crescent moon through the grimy glass window and think to myself, "Maybe Keith is looking at the same moon somewhere in this city. Where is he now?" Soon my eyelids begin to droop. Vaguely I remember telling myself to go back to bed. But when I wake up, I am stretched out across the sofa on my back with sunlight on my face.

◆ ◆ ◆

Niagara Falls, cascading in voluminous and rapid downpours, sends shivers along my spine and raises the hair on my arms. The water roars down from a dizzying height in a sheer drop, splashing into the river below, then rising in fine mists to touch our faces. I stand by the stream above the Falls, watching it churn with relentless determination to tumble over the cliff. The frightening eddies mesmerize me, and like a magnet, pulls me closer to the edge. Through my trancelike state, I see why someone could fall over were it not for the iron fence keeping spectators from harm.

This morning Gabriel and Shirley dropped by, and on the spur of the moment, we all decided to go see the Falls. Jay-Son and I have seen the Falls only in postcards and photographs. I agreed quite enthusiastically as did Jay-Son, who has forgotten his anxiety and now finds every new experience exciting.

"Don't do that," I yell sharply at Jay-Son, who is leaning over the fence. I circle my arm tightly around his waist.

Jay-Son laughs. "You're a scaredy cat." He wriggles to loosen my grip.

But I hang on. "Stop acting silly. You don't horse around at a place like this."

Wen-Lung claps a hand on Jay-Son's shoulder. "Listen to your Mama."

Jay-Son's eyes widen and his mouth trembles. He fights back tears and clamps his lips into a sullen straight line. I lean close to his ear and whisper, "We're just worried that you'll fall over if you're not careful. Don't you see how fast the water is moving and how far down it goes?"

Jay-Son remains stiff. He will have to get used to Wen-Lung reprimanding him. The father figure in his life until a few days ago was his doting grandpa, who never spoke a harsh word to him. He asks in a surly tone, "When are we going back to India?"

Wen-Lung says, "You're living here now."

"I don't like it here. I want to be with my friends." Tears glisten in his eyes.

"We've talked about this before, remember? You'll make lots of new friends when you start school next month."

"Can we go home now?" A soft sob escapes and the voice catches.

"We just got here. We'll eat lunch soon. Don't you want a hot dog? You said you want to try one."

"A hot dog . . . really?" His eyes light up. All is well in Jay-Son's universe again.

"Jay-Son, this is your teacher, Mr McLean," Mrs Lithgow, the school principal, smiles at Jay-Son who stands in stoic silence between Wen-Lung and me.

Red flaming beard bouncing, Mr McLean pumps Jay-Son's hand. "Hello there, you're going to love it here. Do you want to come with me to see your classroom and meet your new friends?"

"Er . . . Mr McLean," I say. "Jay-Son understands very little English."

"Not to worry . . . he won't be the first kid I've taught who doesn't speak English. He'll catch on soon."

Jay-Son's eyes implore me to stay with him as his teacher holds his hand and leads him away. I blink back tears, give him an encouraging smile, and watch him take small steps down the hallway. A few doors away, Jay-Son turns his head in our direction before he enters the classroom. I resist the urge to run after him.

Wen-Lung says with forced lightness, "He'll be fine."

Mrs Lithgow's chin wobbles in agreement. "Don't worry, Mrs Chen. Jay-Son will make new friends soon. Before you know it, he'll be bringing them to your home."

"Thank you, Mrs Lithgow. I hope the other kids won't make fun of him because he doesn't speak English yet."

"Mr McLean will watch over him. He's an experienced teacher."

Wen-Lung nudges my elbow. "I guess we should leave now."

We walk the short distance back to our apartment and enter the elevator in uncomfortable silence. Without Jay-Son's presence and childish chatter to bridge the chasm, we find it hard to relate. I keep telling myself it will take time, but how long?

Back home, I put my handbag on a shelf in the coat closet, pull up a chair and open the newspaper we just bought on the dining table. My familiarity with our space is still tinged with a sense that nothing belongs to me. Maybe it's because I had no part in furnishing it, whereas my imprint was there in every nook of our humble home in Tangra. How I miss Mrs Wong!

Wen-Lung says, "Shall we go shopping when the stores open? I don't have to be at work until this afternoon. Do you need anything before you start your new job?"

My stomach tightens at the reminder. My first job in Canada. "I don't think so. I have enough clothes and Shirley told me not to bring lunch on my first day."

A few days ago, Shirley introduced me to her boss, having heard about an opening at her office. She works at an insurance company. Mr White hired me as his secretary on the spot.

The phone rings. I walk over to the kitchen counter and lift the receiver off the wall phone. "Hello," I say, but there's no response.

"Hello," I say again. Still no answer, and then a child's voice in the background. The phone clicks, and the caller has hung up.

"Who was that?" Wen-Lung asks.

"I don't know. They didn't say anything."

"Must be a prank call. It happens sometimes."

I shrug and go back to the newspaper. A financial crisis is on, and interest rates are soaring to unheard-of heights. At some point this will impact us, I think.

"Maylei."

I look up.

"Do we need more milk?"

"Let me check." I get up and open the fridge. "I didn't realize we're completely out of milk."

"Shall I go down to the store and get some?"

"Don't bother. I'll go later today."

"I'm not doing anything right now. It's no bother."

"Sure, if you want to."

I watch him leave wondering at the change in his attitude. The Wen-Lung of Tangra rarely went to the market, and then only when I was sick. It warms my heart to see that he's trying hard to make our relationship work. It's been a month since I came and so far we have avoided talking about his immigration ordeal and the white woman who helped him become a legal resident. I also stay away from discussing the death of our baby. Feelings of guilt continue to plague me, that beautiful, serene face haunts me even now. He tried to bring up the topic once, but fearing my inability to control my feelings, I changed the subject.

Later Wen-Lung walks in with a jug of milk. His naturally red face is ruddier than usual.

"Are you okay?" I ask.

He glances sharply at me. "Of course, I'm fine. The stupid cashier made me wait a long time in the line."

He's far from fine.

◆ ◆ ◆

Our lives hum along like clockwork. Jay-Son has settled into his new routine and can't stop talking about school and his new friends.

"Mom, can I go play with Benji?"

"Which one is he?"

"He lives in the building over there." He points. "Can I, please?"

It's Sunday morning and I walk Jay-Son to Benji's place. Holding hands, we stroll along the pavement and soak in the autumn sunshine. There's a chill in the air. I step out of Benji's building with a bounce and an urge to explore. It's perfect walking weather. The streets are quiet at this hour. I pick up my pace and let my feet lead me in the neighborhood.

I follow Howard Street out to Parliament and end up on Bloor Street. Across the road I notice a cemetery, and a shiver runs through me. The place looks well maintained, and I chide myself for being silly. I pause for a moment, and then decide to keep walking on Bloor Street, away from the tall buildings. The trees become abundant, their leaves flaming orange, red, and gold. The farther I go, the more vibrant and breathtaking the colors. I come to the bridge overlooking the Don valley and the highway. I lean over the stone railing and look down. My knees tremble and my head spins.

The walk home takes less time. When I pass the entrance to the underground garage, I notice a man and a woman standing just inside the garage, in heated conversation. With shock, I realize that the man is Wen-Lung. As I watch, he grabs the woman's wrist. She flinches, pulls her arm back, and tosses her head. Her face is hidden from my view.

I start walking towards them with partly articulated thoughts and a sinking feeling in the pit of my stomach. A few yards from them, I tell myself to run away. I hesitate. Wen-Lung glances in my direction, and his eyes widen and his mouth hangs open in mid-sentence. The woman turns and stares at me.

"Maylei, what are you doing here?" Wen-Lung has found his voice.

"Oh, I'm sorry, I didn't mean to—"

"This must be *the wife*." The woman's lips curl with contempt.

"Uh, yes, this is my wife." Wen-Lung nods miserably with a caged-animal expression.

"Well, I can see why you're still smitten by her," she says with a sneer. "My name is Megan, and you should thank me for making it possible for you to live in Canada."

I mumble, "Oh, I had no idea you're the woman my husband married." I could have laughed at my words.

Wen-Lung slides his hands in and out of his jean pockets.

"Megan wanted to see me."

I go closer, my initial confusion now replaced by curiosity and an emotion I can't analyze. Sticking my hand out I say, "I'm pleased to meet you."

"Likewise, I'm sure." Megan ignores my gesture and tucks a few short strands of auburn hair behind her ear.

"Mommy," a child yells behind me. A little boy—no more than two years old—runs up to Megan and grabs one of her hands. "Let's go," he says and tugs hard. His upturned face, looking straight at me, sends a shockwave through me. He looks, undeniably, half Chinese. The eyes, the dark hair. The resemblance to Wen-Lung is uncanny—the narrow forehead tapering down to a pointed chin.

Wen-Lung and I look at each other. He sighs and says, "This is Ryan, Megan's son."

"Yours too, Winston, don't you ever forget that, especially when it's time to make your monthly payments."

Winston. He even has a new name to go with this hidden identity. Wen-Lung pushes his hands into his pockets. "I told you I'll provide for him. You don't have to keep reminding me. I'm just a bit short this month because of all the extra expenses."

"Well, that's not my concern. You certainly weren't thinking about these expenses *then*." She emits a harsh laugh.

I whip around and stomp away. Wen-Lung calls after me, "Wait, Maylei. Please let me explain."

I start running. I want to put as much distance as I can from myself and these two people. My world has been shattered with one brief encounter. My breath squeezes out in painful gasps. I cannot contain my anger and grief. I had hoped, foolishly, that the fake marriage was really fake. Yet how could it have been, having gone on for almost two years. Now I am forced to confront my feelings about sharing my husband with a woman in the name of immigration to Canada.

A month ago, I came to Canada filled with hope for our new lives. Now I find myself kicking a Coca-Cola can on the road, wishing it were Wen-Lung. I want to crush it the way he and Megan crushed my hopes moments ago. If only I could hide somewhere and stew in my humiliation.

· 15 ·

"Maylei, listen to me. You know I had to marry Megan so I could stay. I thought I could keep it all businesslike, but it got out of hand. Once my immigration papers were finalized, I'd pay her a lump sum—that was the deal. She seemed really nice when we were introduced to each other. I wish the baby didn't happen."

"You wish he wasn't born or that you didn't sleep with her?"

"Both, of course."

"So when did you decide to start sleeping with her?"

"I never meant for it to happen. It was just the one time. She came to my room one evening when I was feeling really low. We had to live together and pretend to be a real couple. We shared her apartment and split the rent. You have no idea what I went through to bring you and Jay-Son here."

"And you have no idea the different hells I've been through these last five years while you were sleeping with another woman." Does he expect me to believe that they lived together for so long and there was only one transgression? "I was lonely too, but I stayed true to our marriage. The money was always tight. It was no holiday for me. And I would be the pity of Tangra. A laughing stock and failure."

Wen-Lung's face turns a deeper shade of red. "What did you want me to do? If I left Canada and went back to you in India, I wouldn't be able to come back again."

I shake my head, wishing I could dislodge the heaviness I feel in my chest. He still doesn't understand that the price we paid was too high. "I was prepared to give up our dream of immigrating so we could be together as a family again. Our baby died while you were here. I wanted to die. I needed you, but you weren't there. It was the darkest time of my life. And when Jay-Son got sick and had to be hospitalized, I thought I couldn't carry on any more."

"Oh, Maylei, surely you don't blame me for the baby's death? I was just as sad as you to lose her."

"Really? Then you should have acted like a bereaved father. No, I'm not blaming you for her death. With or without you, the same thing would likely have happened. I needed you to be my husband, to be our baby's father, in India, not here. And now to find out that you've fathered a son with another woman. How can I stay with you knowing that you slept with her while you were married to me?"

"Please, Maylei. I know what I did was wrong. How can I make things right for us? Please stay. If not for me, then stay for Jay-Son."

Ah, Jay-Son. My precious son, asleep in his own room, a room he wouldn't have if we lived in Tangra. Perhaps I'm judging Wen-Lung too harshly. Can I look past his cheating and start all over again? Do I have a choice? I don't wish to uproot Jay-Son yet again so soon after our arrival. I take a deep breath, then exhale slowly before answering. "Promise me that you will not see Megan or have anything more to do with her."

A shadow crosses his face. "I want to be rid of her too, but the law is the law. We have a son together, and under the terms of our divorce I have to pay her child support."

"Why didn't you tell me all of this before?"

"How could I? You wouldn't understand. I mean, look at you now."

"Think about the way I found out, Wen-Lung," I give him an icy stare.

"I was hoping that you would never find out," he mumbles. "As long as I kept paying her, we would have been fine. But the last cheque I sent to her bounced because I had spent money on all this furniture." He makes a sweeping gesture with his hands. "It wasn't cheap getting this place ready for you two."

I sense my resolve weakening and try to shore it up one more time. "Still, it was wrong of you to not say anything to me. I don't know if I can ever trust you again."

"Just give me the chance to prove to you that I can be a good husband."

I hear the sincerity in his voice. Exhaling slowly, I mutter, "Fine, we'll try again," and pray silently that I am not making a mistake.

◆ ◆ ◆

Now that Megan and her son are no longer a divisive secret between Wen-Lung and me, I try to focus on the positive aspects of our marriage. I feel fortunate to be living in Canada, where Jay-Son is now adapting to a new life.

The first snowfall arrives in November and nothing can keep Jay-Son inside. He drags me downstairs to play in the white wonderland.

"Mom, watch me," he says and sticks his tongue out to catch the snowflakes.

Flurries dance, frolicking in all directions around us. Jay-Son laughs. I too turn my face up and open my mouth wide, let the snow land on my tongue, tickling it. It all feels magical. Everywhere I look, fluffy flakes swirling in the air, landing gently on the ground, now covered in winter white. Despite the cold, a toasty glow burns inside me. Jay-Son dashes around, hands stretched out like wings. If I had any misgivings about our new life in Canada, they are dissolving right here, right now.

I want to freeze this moment, wish it to last and last, but it's time to go and I call out to Jay-Son.

"Mom, I told you to call me Jay."

"Alright, Jay, it's time to go back up."

Back inside the apartment, I hang up my coat and Jay-Son's snow suit to dry. Just then there's a knock on the door. "Are you expecting anyone?" I ask Wen-Lung.

He shakes his head with a puzzled frown. I peep through the cat's eye. Gabriel's face looms in front of me. I pull the door back. "Gabriel, come on in. This is a surprise. Is Shirley okay?"

Gabriel beams as he walks past me. "Shirley is fine. She just gave birth to a baby girl. I am now a father."

"Congratulations!" Wen-Lung and I exclaim together. "Are we allowed to visit them at the hospital?" I ask.

"Yes, of course." Gabriel's mouth is arranged in a permanent grin and his eyes shine with new-found fatherly love. "You should see how adorable she is."

"I'm sure she's beautiful, just like her parents," I gush. "Can I get you something to drink? Tea or Coke?"

"Thanks, Maylei, but I can't stay. I only came to tell you the good news."

Wen-Lung claps his hand on Gabriel's shoulder. "Get some sleep, man. You look like you need it. I guarantee that you'll be staying up a lot from now on."

Gabriel laughs sheepishly.

After the door closes behind Gabriel, I open the fridge to take out some vegetables. Clutching a bunch of celery, I straighten up, turn around and find myself face to face with Wen-Lung. Tenderness wells up inside me, something I haven't felt in a long time. I touch his arm with my free hand. "I have to tell you something."

His face blanches.

"Oh no, don't look like that. It's good news . . . at least I think it is." I pause and then blurt out, "I may be pregnant."

Wen-Lung's jaw drops. Have I misjudged him? I thought he would be happy with the news. Then his eyes crinkle, and

I exhale with relief.

"When?" he asks.

"I don't know yet, but I've missed one cycle and I'm almost certain because I know the feeling. I'll make an appointment to see the doctor next week."

"So Gabriel isn't the only one with good news today." He puts his hand on my stomach. "I'm thrilled about this. Shall we tell him?" He jerks his head toward Jay-Son whose eyes are glued to the TV screen.

"No, let's wait until I have seen the doctor."

He squeezes my hand. I feel real joy for the first time in many years. The new life forming inside me already fills me with happiness. Then a fleeting ache grips me, a sadness I can never dismiss—always brimming near the surface, reminding me of my loss and utter devastation. I brush aside all negative thoughts because I know that this time everything will be different in a good way.

◆ ◆ ◆

Grace is born in early August, just over a year after Jay-Son and I arrived in Canada.

When I hold her for the first time—pink faced, eyes scrunched, and little mouth open—tears stream down my face. I count her tiny fingers as they curl around mine, and I think that I will burst with all the love swelling inside me. I look forward to my four months of maternity leave—a wonderful Canadian perk that I will experience for the first time.

Wen-Lung visits me at the hospital whenever he can, and I feel spoiled by the devotion he showers upon me. One evening he brings Jay-Son to the hospital. We enter the nursery and stand by Grace's crib. I watch Jay-Son's face anxiously. He strokes her cheeks and makes cooing noises at her. When she smiles, he turns to look at me with eyes as round as saucers. Then she puckers her mouth and belts out a deafening wail. He backs away and I laugh as I lift Gracie into my arms.

Two days after her birth, we bring Grace home. She sleeps on a crib in our bedroom, and very quickly I realize that Jay-Son is jealous of all the attention heaped upon the baby. I ask Wen-Lung to pay more attention to Jay-Son, perhaps take him out to a fun place. Without hesitation Wen-Lung agrees and takes him to Wonderland. Jay-Son is now the happiest kid.

Jay-Son bounces along the sidewalk as I follow behind pushing Grace in the stroller. We're headed for his friend Michael's house, where he will play something called Atari. He can't contain himself and rounds the corner ahead of me. As I follow and make the turn, a boy bumps violently into the stroller. I jolt to a stop and Grace starts to cry.

A woman rushes up and snarls, "Ryan, watch where you're going!" Then she looks at me and steps back. "Oh, it's you."

After the initial shock, my brain registers recognition too. I met Megan once, a year ago. She has a square face framed by the same page-boy cut I now recall. Her scornful look sends a chill into my blood despite the perspiration breaking out on my brow. The thin-lipped mouth that had sneered at me before now volleys expletives I prefer not to repeat.

Avoiding a confrontation, I mutter, "Sorry."

I catch up to Jay-Son, who is watching us with a curious expression. He asks, "Mom, who was that woman?"

"Uh, nobody. Just ignore her."

"I've seen her and the boy before. That woman was talking to Dad at Wonderland. She was there with her son."

I catch my breath. "Are you sure?"

"Of course, I'm sure. Dad gave the boy an ice cream. He was laughing with her."

"And where were you?"

"I was on the merry-go-round. Dad didn't want to go because

he thought it would make him sick."

I feel faint and a queasy sensation grips my stomach. What does this mean? Megan sharing a laugh with Wen-Lung? There must be an explanation for this.

After leaving Jay-Son at his friend's place, I rush home to confront Wen-Lung, but he isn't there. I lift a sleeping Grace out of the stroller, carry her into the bedroom and lay her on the crib. With nothing but my thoughts to distract me now, I let them loose. Any which way I look at it, there can be no explanation for this other than the obvious—Wen-Lung and Megan must have planned the meeting. How long have they been carrying on behind my back? He must have gone back to her while I was pregnant. Probably couldn't keep his fly closed, I seethed. I work myself up into a tizzy, tossing out one explanation after another. And then I hear the front door open.

Wen-Lung's eyes widen when he sees me. "Oh, I didn't know you were home."

"Oh? Does that surprise you?"

"I thought you wanted to stay out a bit and enjoy the weather." He brushes past me and closes the bathroom door. I feel certain that he met Megan downstairs when he thought I was gone.

A few minutes later he emerges and says with a wide smile, "What are you making for lunch today?"

I ignore his question. "You met Megan at Wonderland."

His face clouds briefly, then he gives me a blank stare. "What do you mean by that?"

"I want to know why you didn't tell me about your meeting with Megan last Sunday."

"Uh . . . I didn't want to bother you with more of my problems."

"They couldn't be problems if you were laughing with her."

Wen-Lung's face turns deep red. "Are you accusing me of something?"

"I don't know. You tell me what you were doing with that

woman. I saw her again nearby today. Did you meet with her just now?"

"No, you're being ridiculous, and nothing happened at Wonderland. It was a coincidence that Megan was there. I ran into her . . . that's all. Now what's for lunch?"

"And laughing with her was a coincidence too? I didn't know that you two were on friendly terms. What could she have said that was so funny?"

A vein throbs on Wen-Lung's right temple. "Now you're really annoying me. I told you that we bumped into each other. We don't always have to be angry every time we meet. I tried to be nice to her so she won't bother us, and this is the thanks I get from you."

I mull over his response. "What about this morning? Did you see her again?"

"I told you, I didn't see her. And if I did, I would be nice to her again, so stop looking for something that isn't there."

Although I don't believe he didn't meet her this morning, his last comment makes me feel like a jealous and paranoid wife, which I realize I probably am. "I'm sorry. After the way Megan has behaved, I don't have any good thoughts about her." I sigh. "Maybe you're right, it's better to win her over with kindness than to antagonize her."

Wen-Lung stares at me with a sullen face. "Of course I'm right. Don't be so quick to judge."

· 17 ·

"Maylei, you look well," Our Tangra neighbor Mr Lee's youngest son, Yu-Sen is standing at the door and I am astonished. He hands a small package to me.

"Yu-Sen! When did you arrive in Toronto?"

"Last Saturday. I am called John now." He turns to the man beside him, who has a wide-toothed smiling face. "Do you know my eldest sister's husband Fred? They used to live near New Market in Calcutta."

I remember Fred. He and his wife, Siu-Chin, had dropped by when I first arrived in Toronto. I had brought a parcel from Mrs Lee for them.

We shake hands, and I ask the two men to sit down. Soon Wen-Lung arrives, beaming and wiping his hands on his trousers. The three men need no introductions and before long they're talking about the latest goings-on in Tangra and Calcutta. While I pour Coca-Cola into four glasses, John tells a story about how the monsoon this past summer killed a rickshaw puller in Calcutta. One moment the man was wading through the flooded street, the next he had disappeared down an open manhole. A tragic end to the poor man's life.

And we muse about how fortunate we are to be here in Toronto, how arduous and unfair the immigration process can be, and how we miss Tangra. We talk about the other Chinese here, from Hong Kong and the mainland, and how different we are from them, and also how similar. We all agree that our spicy food is much more exciting.

As soon as John and Fred walk out the door, I rush to open my mother's package. First I pull out an envelope. Wen-Lung watches me while I unfold the parchment-thin paper inside and read the letter. After a short silence he asks, "What does it say?"

"Mother has breast cancer. Father says that he's embarrassed to ask, but he has to borrow some money from us for Mother's surgery."

"How much does he need?"

"One thousand dollars."

"We can't afford that kind of money."

"I have to help them."

"Where will you get the money from?"

"I've been putting away a little bit from my paycheques."

Wen-Lung's face blanches. He knows I've been hiding my bank account from him. Quickly I add, "I thought it would be wise to put aside something for emergencies. A few years ago in India, my savings were wiped out completely after Jay-Son's surgery, and I told myself then that I would never let that happen again."

"I still don't think we can afford to give that money away."

"This is my mother we're talking about. You've been giving money to Megan for how long now? That's money we could be saving to buy a house."

"That's different. I have a legal requirement to pay her, and Ryan . . ."

"This is my mother we're talking about." Now that I've opened the floodgates, I can no longer hold back my thoughts. "You've turned our lives into this mess all because of that woman."

Red-faced, he says, "Do you think we would be here today if it weren't for Megan?"

"And you still believe that I wanted you to do that so we could immigrate? When was I given an opportunity to say no to your fake marriage?" A wave of fury overcomes me, and I'm shaking.

"I didn't hear you say anything about stopping the immigration process." He snarls back.

"What's happened to you? It's like you're no longer the same person I married."

"Well, I went through a lot here and that can change a person. You're not the same either!"

"Like the hell you went through romancing one wife here while keeping the other in the dark."

"Tell me you don't want to live here. Why don't you just leave now and go back to Tangra!" Spittle foams at the corners of his mouth.

"Why? So you can continue to fool around with Megan like you're doing even now?" I fling the words at him, no longer caring of the outcome.

Wen-Lung inches closer to me, "Watch what you're saying. You wanted to come to Canada too, but you won't admit it."

"Not as much as you wanted it. I never asked you to get married to that woman. That was your idea, and now we're stuck with paying her."

"And you're benefiting from all my hard work now."

"What benefit? Half your pay goes to Megan. I'm keeping us afloat right now. And I don't hear you denying that you're still seeing her."

"I haven't admitted to anything."

"You haven't denied anything either."

"Mom, Dad, stop fighting." Jay-Son jumps up from the sofa, where he's been watching us, and storms off into his bedroom. Gracie howls at the same time.

My shoulders slump and all the fight leaves me. I am ashamed for losing my temper and saying what I said. I feel empty and sad as I pick up Gracie and follow Jay-Son into his room. He is sitting on his bed, his fists balled and eyes in tears. I pull him toward me whispering, "I'm so sorry you had to hear us like this.

Sometimes parents disagree."

Jay-Son buries his face into my shirt and sobs. I glance up and see Wen-Lung watching us from the doorway, his lips clamped into a straight thin line. I plead with my eyes, but I don't know what I'm pleading for. Do I want him to deny that he's having an affair with Megan? Do I want him to agree to give money to my parents?

But I no longer care what Wen-Lung thinks. For too long I have buried my head, unwilling to look at the inevitable. To pick up a marriage after a separation of five years was a daydream. Madness. It was broken even before I arrived. Only Jay-Son held it together.

· 18 ·

Wen-Lung and I separated over a year ago. To my surprise, he offered no resistance, and later I found out that he was back with Megan. I haven't heard from him since we parted ways. It was almost too easy.

When my friend Joy Liang offered to become my roommate we moved into a three-bedroom apartment together, in the same building. Joy has been avoiding deportation by keeping a low profile and off the immigration department's radar. Living with a family makes her inconspicuous. All her friends' attempts to find her a suitor with landed status have been unsuccessful so far. At thirty-three, her prospects for marriage don't look good, and the chances of finding a Hakka man is even more remote. I told her jokingly that as a soon-to-be-divorced mother of two, my chances of landing a new husband were even worse.

Inside Sherbourne Station this day, I board a westbound train and get off at Yonge. A northbound train pulls in and I step inside and find a seat. I sit back and glance casually at the window beside me, and suddenly I stop breathing and my heart bounces like a rubber ball against my rib cage. I cannot believe what my eyes see.

Standing at the platform and staring wide-eyed at me, is a face I have not forgotten. Keith waves uncertainly at first, then realizing its really me he mouths my name and rushes toward the door at the same time that I attempt to rise. The door panels slide shut, and as we stare at each other with open mouths, the train begins to move. He jogs alongside saying something I cannot hear and then falls behind hopelessly.

I look at my watch. I cannot afford to go back if I want to keep my doctor's appointment. If I miss this one, I might not get another one for weeks. Free public medicine is nice, but it has its drawbacks. But I shouldn't complain, we came with nothing.

Still, at the next station my legs move on their own, unconsciously. There is a desperate hope inside me. If . . . What if . . . I'm almost in tears. I step onto the platform, and seconds later, I am the lone standing figure there. The door-chime signals the closing of the doors and I dash back towards the train. For a second time, the door shuts in my face. Digging my hands inside my coat pockets, I watch the train disappear into the tunnel.

What do I hope to accomplish? Will Keith come after me? What was he trying to tell me? I don't need any more complications. Inviting him back into my life will cause more pain for us both. That's assuming he's unattached, and we've not changed. But we have. It's been seven years since we last met, and we know how that ended. Yet I'm desperate to see him again, at least to talk to him. But again, this is madness. We broke up ten years ago; life must go on.

When we last met, all the old wounds had opened up and it took months before I recovered. In Canada, I told myself that the best thing to do was to avoid any future contact with Keith. Risking her wrath and our friendship, I did not write to his sister.

The next train pulls up. When it stops, I stand aside and scan the passengers' faces as they stream out. No Keith.

◆ ◆ ◆

This time the loss I feel casts a gloom like a persistent dark cloud over my head, choking the life out of me. Over the next few days, I find myself listless and often lost in my thoughts. I know that my desperation to see Keith is because I am lonely, without a man. I'm pathetic, a dreamer.

"Mom, did you hear what I just said?"

I stare blankly at Jay-Son. "Uh, what was that, sweetie?"

"I was asking if I could bring money for our school trip. We're going to a farm, and our teacher said that we can pick up a pumpkin for Halloween."

"Of course, how much do you need?" I walk over to the closet and reach up the shelf for my handbag.

"A dollar," he says. "Mom, can we carve the pumpkin when I bring it home?"

I retrieve my wallet. I don't really understand why Canadians carve pumpkins for Halloween, but I say, "Sure."

Jay-Son eyes me with a strange look. "Will you help me carve it?"

I hand him the money. "Of course, dear."

"Are you okay, Mom?"

"I'm fine. Why do you ask?"

"You're not paying attention," he says peevishly.

I shake myself out of my stupor. "Oh, Jay-Son, I'm so sorry. Tell me what's going on with you. I promise I'll listen."

He shrugs, rolls his eyes, and starts to tickle his sister who is holding on to the sofa's edge testing her walking skills. I watch him laugh as Gracie lands on her diapered bottom, then gurgles and giggles. Tears prick my eyelids. Jay-Son does get along with Gracie these days and no longer feels threatened by her.

My gaze falls on the telephone directory on the bottom panel of the coffee table. If Joy were here, maybe she would reason me out of what I'm about to do. But she's gone out with friends, and I feel sad and lonely tonight. I lug the three-inch phone book to the kitchen counter and flip the pages until I reach W. Keith Wilson is listed several times along with one K Wilson. I fold the top corner of the page and close the book. Then I put the kids to bed.

Heart thumping, I open the bookmarked page in the directory, pick up the phone and dial the first name on my list. After three rings, a woman answers, "Hello."

"Uh, I'm looking for Keith Wilson." My voice sounds shaky and squeaky.

"Keith . . . there's a call for you," the woman yells.

I hold my breath as I wait. A male voice says, "Hello."

"Sorry, wrong number." I hang up the phone. Now that the first call is out of the way, I go through the entire list with more confidence. But not one of them belongs to my Keith. Why do I still say *my*? That's how desperate I am. Frustrated, I close the book. Stop this foolishness, I tell myself. I drum my fingers on the kitchen counter. Not finding Keith is a good thing; it is a sign not to touch the past. Why would any man want to rekindle a relationship with an old flame who, as far as he knows, is still married? He wouldn't appreciate a neurotic ex-girlfriend calling him.

What if he's also looking for me? Can he find me? He will be searching for Wen-Lung's name in the phone book. I start to flip the phone pages again. At the bookmarked place, I thumb through the list. This time my eyes fall on "Wilson S K." My breath catches. This must be him. His first name is Stanley, I know that, but he disliked it so much that he rarely told anyone about it. I feel certain that I have the right number. Almost. I dial the number.

"Hello," a woman's voice floats through the wires.

This is a bad idea. He must be married. "Oh, may I speak to Keith?"

"Hold on . . . Keith, there's a call for you."

The voice in my head screams at me to hang up the phone, but my brain has lost its power over my fingers.

"Hello." Keith's unmistakable voice. I think I will swoon.

Then panic sets in. What have I done? Who was that woman? His wife? His girlfriend? I put down the phone without uttering a word, stagger to a chair and flop down. What am I doing? If Keith is married I can't barge into his life like that. Maybe that's why he didn't come when he saw me on the train. Did I mistake the confusion on his face then?

When I feel more normal I look down at the phone book still open on the bookmarked page. I read Keith's address, and on an impulse, I search for the map inside the coffee table drawer. Like a stalker I thumb through the street names, find the grid and locate Keith's street. It's at Yonge and Sheppard, a thirty-minute ride away. Knowing where he lives gives me a certain sense of satisfaction. I can now place him somewhere in this vast city.

· 19 ·

The urge to hear his voice draws me to the phone like a moth to a light bulb. Several times at work, my hand reaches for the phone, but each time I find enough strength to stop myself. My emotional tug-of-war continues at home. Jay-Son and Gracie went to bed half an hour ago, and I can hear Joy taking a shower. I pick up the phone for the umpteenth time, glance furtively around the room, and this time I allow my fingers to dial the number already committed to memory.

After a few rings, the phone gets picked up and I hear Keith's voice.

"Keith?"

"Maylei? Is that you?"

There's no turning back now. "Yes. How are you?"

"Maylei, I've been searching for you ever since I saw you at the subway station."

"You have?"

"Of course. I was on my way to a meeting before heading home. After I saw you, the next train couldn't come fast enough for me. I took a spot in the first car so I could scan every platform that we passed, but I didn't see you. If I'd seen you I would have got off and skipped the meeting. I was devastated that I lost you again."

I want to sing out loud. He did come for me. I mumble, "I'm glad I found you."

"Glad? I'm ecstatic you've found me. You've done a really good job of disappearing in Toronto. I searched the phone book for Wen-Lung Chen but found nothing. Then I called Astrid to see if she had your number or address, but she said you never wrote to her. Let me warn you that she's more than a little upset with you. I can't guarantee your safety when she sees you." A soft chuckle follows.

"I didn't mean to hurt her . . . I . . . I'll write and apologize."

"Tell me what you've been up to since you came to Toronto. I want to know everything."

"I'm working as a secretary in an insurance company. What about you?" I want to know if he's married, but I'm afraid to ask.

"I'm with a bank, the same company I started with when I first arrived here. I'm a senior developer now. Listen, Maylei, is it possible for us to meet?"

"Meet? How . . . where?"

Is it wise to see him again? Who was that woman who answered the phone yesterday?

"How about lunch tomorrow?"

"That woman . . . your wife—"

He laughs. "Were you my prank caller last night?" He pauses. "I'm not married."

I can barely conceal the giddiness from my voice. "I thought that woman was your wife, and I didn't want to disturb you."

"You have no idea how happy I am that you decided to call again."

"Not happier than I am."

I hear a sharp intake of his breath. "So how about meeting for lunch tomorrow? . . . assuming it's okay with Wen-Lung."

"Wen-Lung and I are separated."

"Oh, I can't wait to see you again."

◆ ◆ ◆

I sense his presence behind me, before I actually lay eyes on him.

The faint musky scent—do I imagine it? I turn around and look into his eyes. For a brief moment, nothing and no one exists except for the two of us. He murmurs my name. He grasps my hands. He leans forward, brushes his lips against my cheek.

The old Maylei would have surely swooned at the nearness, the touch and the sound of his voice, but too much water has washed and bumped over these rocky ten years for us to remain the same. And so, although my heart beats faster at the wonder of this moment I stay outwardly composed. "Keith, it's been a long time."

He tightens his grip around my hands. "It's so good to see you."

A hostess beckons us to follow her. Keith holds on to my hand and the pressure of his palm against mine is the only sensation I can focus on. At the table, I reluctantly let go of his hand and slide into my seat.

"How are you doing? How's your son, Jay-Son, is it?"

"Jay-Son is fine . . ."

"He must be a big boy now. How old is he?"

"He turned nine recently."

A shadow crosses his face. "The last time we met in Calcutta you were pregnant. Was it a girl or a boy?"

I have been expecting this question, and don't answer. Keith says, "I'm sorry. I can see that something is wrong."

"I guess Astrid never told you that my baby was stillborn. She was beautiful and perfectly formed."

He reaches for my hands across the table. "Oh, Maylei, don't look so sad. I can't bear to see you like this."

I take a deep breath and blink back my tears. "It was the worst time of my life, even worse than . . . I didn't think I could survive the pain. And yet, here I am. Had she lived, she would have been seven."

"And Wen-Lung was here the whole time while you were going through all that," he says.

"It took longer than we anticipated. But maybe it's not such a good idea to talk about it. That part of my life is over. I'm here, aren't I? I wouldn't be, otherwise!"

Keith puts his fork down. "Why did you leave Wen-Lung?"

Over food we talk about everything except what's on our minds. Is he committed, I want to know? There is no doubt in my mind that he still has feelings for me—but is that enough? We are no longer the same people we were ten years ago. We are both in our thirties now.

"Wen-Lung and I split up over a year ago, a few months after our daughter was born. I found out something about him." I want to tell him about Megan and her son, but maybe it's too soon.

His eyes search my face. "Are you happy?"

I shrug. "I'm as happy as I can be." Now I look up and watch his face closely. "You never told me who that woman was who picked up the phone the first time I called you."

"Why is that important?"

"Oh, I'm just curious," I reply a little too sharply.

"That's all?" His voice mocks me. "That was Leslie, my cousin Nevil's wife. They live with me."

Is that relief I am feeling?

"What about girlfriends?" I ask keeping a straight face.

Keith furrows his brow and purses his lips. I sense that he is struggling with some difficult emotions. Quickly I say, "I'm sorry, perhaps I shouldn't have asked."

Giving a thin-lipped smile he says, "Don't be sorry, Maylei. About a year ago my fiancée took off with someone I considered a good friend. They got married shortly after. Needless to say, I wasn't invited to that wedding."

"Oh no, I'm sorry," I say again. Conflicting feelings of sadness and joy play havoc with my head and my heart.

"It's okay, I've had enough time to recover, and sometimes the universe works in strange ways. Maybe things will work out for the better." This time his smile lifts the corners of his mouth.

I laugh nervously. "I hope so. Let me show you a photo of Jay-Son and Gracie."

Keith takes the picture from my hand and looks at the happy faces of my children. After a long pause, he stares at me with a strange expression. "They're good looking kids. Gracie looks like you, but Jay-Son . . . who does he take after?"

"He looks just like his dad."

"His dad . . . hmm. I never met Wen-Lung."

"It's better that way." I put the picture back inside my purse.

· 20 ·

The words couldn't have echoed more loudly in my head than if Jinlei had spoken them aloud to me. I stare at her letter in my hand. Mother appears to be free from cancer, she says, but continues to be concerned about me. What does she mean?

The telephone rings and without looking up, I reach for the receiver on the wall.

"Hello, Maylei."

"Oh, Keith, it's so good to hear from you." I can't hide the relief from my voice, as worry for my mother slips from my mind.

"Did you miss me that much?"

"You have no idea how much."

"What do you think about bringing your children to spend a day at my house tomorrow?"

My throat makes a strange sound before I come up with, "Gracie has been very fussy. She may be coming down with something. I'm not sure how she'll behave in a strange place." That's true, but my real reason for not wanting to go to Keith's house has got nothing to do with Grace, and everything to do with Jay-Son.

"Oh, that's too bad. Then would you like to go for dinner tomorrow? I'll pick you up at your place."

I glance at Jay-Son who seems absorbed with writing his journal for a school assignment. "Let me check with Joy to see if she'll look after the kids."

"I'll pick you up around six tomorrow."

As I hang up the phone, I watch Jay-Son frowning in deep

concentration over his notebook. I see his father in his eyes, and in the brown wavy locks falling carelessly over his forehead.

I go and knock on Joy's door. "Come in," she calls out.

Joy is sitting propped up against the headboard by a couple of pillows, a Chinese novel opened on her lap. I sit down on the bed and move closer to her. "Do you remember years ago before Wen-Lung and I got married, I told you about Keith and me?"

She closes her book and wrinkles her brow. "Yeah, I remember. You were madly in love with him, but your parents wanted you to marry Wen-Lung instead."

"Look how well that's turned out." I grimace. "Keith lives in Toronto now. I bumped into him accidentally a few weeks ago, and we've met a few times since then."

"You sneaky little thing . . . I'm so happy for you. I knew there was something different about you these past few weeks, but I couldn't put my finger on it."

"I should have told you before, but I didn't want to say anything too soon in our relationship. It's like I'm getting a second chance with Keith, and I have to pinch myself sometimes to remind myself that this is real."

"If anyone deserves a second chance, you do. But what about your parents? Do they know?"

"You're the first person I'm telling. My parents won't be happy, but I'm not seeking their approval anymore. I don't need their permission to date someone." Even as I say this with all the confidence that I can muster, I hear Jinlei's voice in my head reproaching me for leaving my marriage. She writes whenever she feels motivated enough to pick up a pen after putting her four young children to bed and finishing her endless chores.

My parents are still unhappy about my separation. Women in Tangra are blaming me and Mother wants me to go back to Wen-Lung.

Joy asks, "Keith never married all this time?"

"No, that's the crazy part. He almost did once, but his fiancée married someone else instead. He says he still loves me. I'm so glad he's still single, and I don't care that he's only half Chinese. If only I had been strong enough to insist to my parents all those years ago."

"Well, Maylei, you go for it this time. Don't let anything stand in the way. Any man who's waited this long for you must surely be someone special. I'll back you up all the way with this one."

She looks pensive. Here I am, gloating about Keith when she just broke up with her boyfriend. And she doesn't have legal status. I lean forward and squeeze her hand.

◆ ◆ ◆

Keith knocks on the door at six and I breathe a sigh of relief because Joy and the children are still not home. I told Joy to take her time. Although I want Keith to meet my children, I'm not ready for that yet.

A smiling Keith greets me at the door, looking like the perfect date. Butterflies seem to dance in my stomach, as I step aside and invite him in. He grasps my arms, bends his head, and pecks my cheek. His short beard brushes against my skin, and I inhale the familiar musky scent. The butterflies calm down.

"You look beautiful tonight," he says.

I smooth my hands self-consciously over my red polyester shirt tucked inside a pair of black trousers. "You're not too shabby yourself," I reply, trying to act composed.

"Where are your children?"

"Joy took them to the variety store so Gracie won't cry when she sees me leave."

A look of disappointment crosses his face. "Oh, I was looking forward to meeting them. Shall we wait for them to return?"

"I'm not sure how long they'll be. Let's go before the restaurant gets busy."

"You're right. Perhaps I'll see them next time."

When we arrive at Sai Woo, Keith's favorite Chinese restaurant, the second floor is teeming with people. There is a clamor of voices as waiters weave in and out between tables and slap plates and cutlery on the plastic-covered tables.

I pay no attention to the food in front of us. Instead, I'm fascinated with how Keith handles his chopsticks. Jay-Son holds them upright almost like two pencils poised to write, the same way that Keith is holding his. Am I imagining this in my enthusiasm?

The waiter brings us the bill, and Keith pays. "Maylei, let's go to my place. I'll make you the best cup of chai you'll ever taste in Canada. It's as good as the milk tea we used to drink at St Agnes'."

"Will I get to meet your cousin and his wife?"

He grins. "They've gone out for a late movie. They won't come back until after midnight."

My nerves are taut with uncertainty as we drive to Keith's house. Half an hour later, Keith parks his car on the driveway of his bungalow off Yonge Street. Two lantern-shaped fixtures on either side of the front door shed light on the porch and three steps. Keith holds the door open for me and flicks a switch on the inside wall. I step into a small foyer that leads to a spacious living room on my right. Leaving my boots on a tray, I pad in my stockinged feet on the green carpet. Keith helps me out of my coat and drapes it over a chair in the dining room to our left. A few seconds later, I feel his arms slide around my waist from behind. I lean back against him; it feels right and the most natural thing to do.

"I love you, Maylei. I realize I've never stopped loving you."

I turn to face him and look at him in wonder. "I don't know what I've done to deserve you."

After a while we ease our grip on each other and catch our breaths. "Let me make you the tea I promised," he says.

I put a hand on his arm. "Forget the tea. Let's just sit and talk."

Keith leads me to the sofa. He sits beside me, and puts one arm over my shoulders, twirling my hair around his fingers.

"Maylei?"

"Yes . . ."

"Maylei," he murmurs again. "Will you marry me?"

This is everything I want. "Keith," I whisper, "why do you want me? I've been married before, many would consider me used. You can find any number of eligible girls . . . so, why me?"

"Because you're the only person I ever want to marry. Because I didn't fight hard enough for you the first time. Because I made a mistake in letting you go. Now I want to make you mine."

"I have two children already. You've never been married before."

"So I'd be more eligible if I were married at least once?"

"Of course not, that's not what I mean!"

"Do you think I would propose to you if I weren't prepared to be a father to your children?"

Should I, or shouldn't I? I take a deep breath. "Keith, I haven't been completely honest with you. I need to tell you something."

Keith furrows his brow. "Why so serious? You're scaring me."

"Keith, there's no easy way to tell you this." I blurt out, "Jay-Son is your son."

He opens his mouth and widens his eyes. "What—"

"Please don't be upset with me. I can't bear it if you get angry with me."

"Shh . . . Maylei." He puts a finger on my lips. "Why would I be upset? I'm just shocked to find out that Jay-Son is my son. I need to let the news sink in. How do you know . . . And Wen-Lung?"

"When I got pregnant with Jay-Son I thought I was carrying Wen-Lung's baby. I'm sure you remember that Wen-Lung and I got married within a few weeks of our . . . "

"Oh, Maylei, that memory has kept me going all these years." Keith's voice shakes. "I had a strange feeling when I saw Jay-Son's picture."

"I noticed the expression on your face and almost kicked myself for being so careless."

"Does anyone know?"

"I think my parents suspect, but I haven't told anyone."

"If you thought you were pregnant with Wen-Lung's baby, then how did you find out that Jay-Son is mine?"

"Jay-Son was born eight months after I was married. The moment I saw him I knew he couldn't be Wen-Lung's baby. His color and most of his facial features look Chinese, but he has the same brown eyes as yours. No one had any cause to suspect that he wasn't Wen-Lung's son. If someone saw the two of you together, they might have put two and two together and become suspicious. Luckily, only my family and Joy knew about you, but they never met you. We could do a paternity test to be certain . . ."

Keith pulls a tissue from the coffee table and gently wipes my cheeks. "No need for any tests. I take your word for it. I wish I'd known you were pregnant. I would have moved the earth to marry you even though you were a stubborn little thing . . . and you still are."

Mixed emotions chase across his face. A few seconds later he says, "There's a part of me that wants to be mad with you." He squeezes my hand. "But what would that achieve? I love you with or without Jay-Son. Now there's even more reason for us to get married. But will he accept me? If I could turn the clock back, I'd want to see him as a baby, as a toddler, and as he grows."

"I never intended to hurt you like this. After I discovered the truth about Jay-Son, I decided to guard the secret with my life. You were already gone, and Wen-Lung would have discarded me and turned me out on the street. All the Hakka folks in Tangra would have shunned me and sided with him. What else could I do?"

"Do you think Wen-Lung suspects anything now?"

"No."

Keith mulls over this last bit of information. He rakes his hand through his hair. "So what if someone finds out now? You're separated from Wen-Lung and your divorce is happening."

"Wen-Lung could make things very nasty for us. He may fight for custody of Gracie. It could become an ugly divorce. If I keep you out of the picture, then we have a chance of a quick settlement. He wants to re-marry Megan as soon as possible."

"Re-marry Megan?" He furrows his brow.

I explain to Keith about the circumstances of our immigration, and Wen-Lung's indiscretion.

"I can't wait to see Jay-Son. When can I see him?" I hear his longing. "I don't care where we meet as long as I get to see my son."

Keith and I agree that no one but his immediate family and my friend Joy should know about our engagement until my divorce is finalized. I don't tell even my own family. Wen-Lung has already moved in with Megan.

Today Keith will meet my children for the first time. Despite my protests, he insists on coming to pick us up at the apartment. Snow is in the forecast. I've told Jay-Son we are going to see Uncle Keith.

"Does he have a big house?" he asks.

"It's a nice place," I answer.

When Keith arrives, he stares unabashedly at his son. I watch many emotions chase across his face, and I fear he may be fighting a losing battle with his composure. His voice is unusually gruff as he says, "So this is Jay-Son."

Holding Gracie in one arm I rest a trembling hand on my son's shoulder and say, "Jay-Son, this is Uncle Keith." Such a momentous meeting reduced to mere words. I wonder what Keith is thinking.

Jay-Son sidles closer to me. He glances at me and then at Keith. Curling his mouth into a cautious smile, he says, "Hello Uncle Keith. Everyone calls me Jay at school."

Keith extends an arm out. I clench my teeth and jaws as I watch Jay-Son place a tentative hand on Keith's open palm. Now Jay-Son glances at me and deepens the furrows between his eyebrows. He senses an inexplicable tension. It may be obvious, even to a nine-year-old, that this is not just any meeting with a new uncle.

A lusty cry from Gracie rends the charged air. White fur frames her scrunched pink face, her eyes squeezed shut and mouth wide open.

Keith chuckles, "She sure has a pair of healthy lungs. Let's get going."

Icy sunshine dazzles our eyes when we step outside the building. Keith pauses to slip on his sunglasses. He then clasps Jay-Son's hand, and they walk together in front of me. I put my shades on too and follow closely behind with Gracie. The sidewalk is dry and snow-free for now. Throughout the short walk to Keith's car, parked along the road, I hear Jay-Son volley questions at Keith, his initial shyness forgotten.

We pile into the car. I slide into the back with Gracie and let Jay-Son sit in the front. Keith drops my backpack on the empty seat beside me, and then closes the door. After he has slid into the driver's seat, he glances at Jay-Son, and turns his head to look at me.

Keith parks his car in front of his red brick bungalow. When I was here previously, it was too dark to see the surroundings. Now I notice a large bay window flanked by two six- or seven-foot green pines. Between them sprawls a shrub, its branches leafless for now, in all directions.

As we climb the three steps up the small porch, someone flings the door open and squeals, "Nevil, they're here!"

A woman in light blue sweats over an ample girth stands at the door. Her comely face, framed in short curly black hair breaks into a wide smile as she steps aside. "Come in, come in. You must be Maylei. I'm Leslie Wilson, Nevil's wife. I'm sure you already know that Nevil and Keith are cousins."

The cousin right on cue behind Leslie. "Finally we get to meet you. We were beginning to despair that you might only be a figment of Keith's imagination."

They take turns to embrace us. I struggle out of my coat and then strip Gracie's snow suit off her. From the corner of my eyes I notice Keith helping Jay-Son out of his jacket. Leslie stretches out her arms for Gracie who doesn't take kindly to strangers and shies away with a puckered mouth. Quickly I soothe her before she has a chance to exercise her vocal chords once more.

"Come and sit here, Maylei," Leslie beckons me to the dining room.

I follow her with a sense of fate and its twisted and whimsical ways. I realize that—unbeknownst to her when she answered my initial phone call—this cheerful and bubbly person almost sabotaged my reunion with Keith. She grabs Jay-Son's hand and pulls him toward a chair. "Come sit next to your mama." As Jay-Son perches suspiciously on the seat beside me, she remains standing, tousling his hair. "You're a handsome little boy, Jay-Son." She glances at Keith who is about to sit down across from Jay-Son. Keith flashes a warning look at her and shakes his head ever so slightly.

Taking his seat across the table from me, Nevil says, "Honey, leave the boy alone. You're embarrassing him."

Leslie glares at her husband and says sweetly to Jay-Son. "My dear adorable boy, you're the spitting image of someone I know."

Jay-Son glances at me and nods as if agreeing. "I look like my mom."

"That must be it." Leslie says emphatically and shoots Keith a meaningful glance. "All right, sit back and relax while I bring out the goodies I've prepared."

I breathe a sigh of relief as Leslie disappears into the kitchen. A few minutes later, she returns with a serving bowl filled with large brown gulab jamun, floating in warm sugar syrup. Next she brings out a plate of crispy golden fried samosa, then vegetarian pakora heaped high on another plate, then a small bowl of mixed Indian savories, and finally quarter plates and spoons. Although Keith has already warned me about Leslie's idea of a mid-afternoon snack I am shocked at what I see in front of us. Gesturing at the food, she says, "Come, come, let's eat. Let me get you a samosa." She picks one with a tong, places it on a plate and sets it in front of Jay-Son.

"Leslie, you shouldn't have gone through all this trouble for us," I tell her.

"No trouble at all. I love to cook. I made the gulab jamun last night. Keith told me that it's one of your favorite Indian desserts. This morning I made the samosas. Unlike the cheap potato stuffing you get at the stores, these are stuffed with ground beef."

Nevil chuckles. "Can you tell that Leslie likes to snack?"

Leslie throws him a withering glance. "Look at that belly and tell me who the snacker is."

Rubbing his paunch, Nevil winks at me. "When she cooks, I have to eat. If I don't, she gets mad with me."

Leslie snorts and pats her husband's belly. "Do you know how to cook Indian food, Maylei? Keith's mom used to make great Chinese food for us, but her curries were . . . let's just say we told her to stick with Chinese cooking."

We all laugh.

"Can you spend Christmas with us, Maylei?" Keith asks. "Ask Joy to come too."

Back in India I had attended Christmas Eve mass until I lapsed and stopped observing the event. But now these past couple of Christmases here in Toronto, I decided to celebrate with a special dinner and gifts for the children so that Jay-Son would not feel left out. Now I glance at him, brow wrinkled in concentration over the cards laid out on the dining table. "Jay," I call out, "what do you think about coming here on Christmas?"

He looks up, shrugs, and nods. "Okay, I guess."

"Good," Leslie says. "I will roast a turkey."

"I will bring a Chinese dish and a dessert," I volunteer. "Let me know what I can do to help."

Keith flashes me a happy grin.

· 22 ·

Christmas has come and gone. On the day, we spent the evening feasting on Leslie's turkey and curried stuffing. She used her mother's recipe, reminding Keith of what he'd missed since he left Calcutta. Now Leslie plans to introduce their traditions here in Canada. While I'm happy for Keith that he's reconnecting with his roots, I'm saddened that he must have been lonely, living here all by himself these past ten years.

He seems to be making up for lost time and he can't get enough of us. He wants to come to the apartment to pick us up every Sunday morning to go to his house. As much as I want the same thing, I caution against it. We could bump into someone who knows us or even Wen-Lung. As long as Wen-Lung and I are not divorced, the risk is too great to take.

◆ ◆ ◆

Light snowflakes float around me as I step out of the office building after work. I hum a tune and stride toward the subway station. The January chill is a nuisance. Keith called me earlier to tell me that he would join us for dinner. Sometimes I still pinch my arm to remind myself that he's truly back with me. If not for Wen-Lung and his delay tactics regarding our divorce, my life feels almost charmed. I frown and quickly dismiss negative thoughts.

Forty minutes and two subway trains later, I arrive at my building. The elevator door creaks open just as I am beginning to wonder if I should climb the twelve floors to my babysitter's apartment, which is in the same building. If the rent weren't so affordable and the location so convenient, I would gladly move to a building where the elevators are more reliable.

As I hit the twelfth-floor button, a woman rushes inside. It's Shirley. "Hi," I say with a weak smile.

She reaches for the sixth-floor button, averts her eyes and stares straight ahead. Gabriel's wife, my sewing student in Calcutta, wants nothing to do with me since Wen-Lung and I split up. Gabriel too has been treating me like someone with a contagious disease. I should have known this would happen. The Hakka community still frowns upon divorce, and the blame naturally belongs to me for being ungrateful for all the hardships Wen-Lung had to endure to bring us to Canada.

Shirley crosses her arms and focuses her attention on the door. I stare at the number panel. The elevator chugs up at snail's pace until it shudders and stops at the sixth floor. When Shirley leaves, I breathe a sigh of relief. This will not be the last awkward meeting with her.

A few minutes later I knock on Mrs Liu's door. She beams at me with her round face, and says in Hakka, "Maylei, ah . . . your husband came by to pick up your children already."

My heart lurches and blood drains from my face. Struggling to sound normal I ask, "When did Wen-Lung come for them?"

"He came around four." Mrs Liu frowns. "What's wrong?"

"You do know that my husband and I are separated, right?"

"Yes, but he said that he still sees the kids. They're his too, you know." She sniffs.

Of course, Mrs Liu too disapproves of my situation. She treats me like a familiar neighbor because I knew her from Tangra.

"Please, Mrs Liu, don't let anyone pick up my children unless I've given you permission."

Mrs Liu's layered chin wobbles, and I brace myself for her next words. "You young people don't know how to work things out these days. You split up at the slightest problem. In my days when we got married, we stayed married." She sniffs again. "And why are you worried? Wen-Lung said that he's taking the kids home."

"Whose home?"

"He just said home. Yours, his . . . they should be the same."

I turn on my heels and let myself out of the apartment. My brain conjures up all kinds of images about where Wen-Lung could be taking the children as I race to the fire exit and sprint downstairs to the ninth floor. We have an agreement for him to pick them up every other Saturday. Why did he suddenly decide to come this evening without notice? He knows I don't get home until after five. My mind jumps around anxiously, probably unreasonably. When I reach my door, I hear sounds from the TV. Relief quickly gives way to anger. My hand trembles as I insert the key into the lock.

Although every inch of me wants to storm inside and scream at Wen-Lung, I remove my boots and coat slowly. Wen-Lung and Jay-Son glance up at me from the floor where miniature cars are lined up for a race. I can see that Miss Piggy and Kermit the Frog have been keeping Gracie company, but she now toddles towards me with a toothy grin.

I pick up Gracie into my arms. Then I turn angrily to Wen-Lung. "How did you get the key for this place? You shouldn't have picked up the kids and barged in here without checking with me first."

Wen-Lung smiles in the way I used to find quite endearing when we first met. "I wanted to surprise you and Jay-Son. Since it's Friday I decided to come here straight from work as I can't see the kids tomorrow. Megan and I are taking Ryan to see her parents up north. I saw the superintendent downstairs and told him that I had locked myself out. He let me in without a question." He gives a self-deprecating shrug and looks somewhat shamefaced.

I will not to give in to his charm—a fleeting change of attitude to get his way—and I reply in a frigid tone, "I'll have to speak to him about not doing this again. I don't want you walking in and out of my apartment without my permission. We have a visitation schedule—every other Saturday. You can't keep changing it on a whim. The last few times when you skipped without telling me, I let you off, but you can't just show up any time without checking with me."

Wen-Lung says sarcastically, "Don't worry, Maylei, all will be well in your world. I won't disrupt it again by picking up the children."

"Look, Wen-Lung, I don't mean to sound ungrateful, but wc made a decision to lead separate lives. You can't insert yourself in whenever you feel like it."

I wish I hadn't been so lax with our separation agreement regarding his visits with the children; I did not want a bitter divorce and still don't.

Wen-Lung shrugs into his jacket and heads for the door. "Is this how you want our relationship? I must make an appointment to see my own children? I have my own life . . . want to start one . . . "

"No . . . yes . . . I mean I want you to continue to be a part of their lives, but don't drop in and out without warning."

"If that's how you feel, then certainly, I will call before I come."

I lock the door behind him with a touch of regret and perhaps some guilt. Did I behave unreasonably? Am I just possessive and jealous? He must miss the children.

Keith will be here in another hour. I put aside all thoughts of Wen-Lung, and say a silent prayer of thanks that the two men have not crossed paths yet.

· 23 ·

Joy buttons her coat, glances at me and grins. "Maylei, would you mind locking the door after me? I'm running a bit late for the movie. Nancy is waiting for me downstairs."

I hold the doorknob while she breezes past me into the hallway outside. "Have fun," I call out to her.

Joy waves and her long steps take her to the elevators in a few seconds. As I lock the door, I almost regret turning down her suggestion to go to the theatre with her. I thought Gracie would be tired and prove to be a handful so close to her bedtime. I wonder if Keith is home yet from his business trip to New York City. He has tagged on an extra day to go sightseeing and should be back this evening. He promised to come tomorrow, as usual, for his weekly visit. The sound of Gracie whimpering interrupts my thoughts. She scatters the Lego blocks in front of her with uncharacteristic force just as Jay-Son jumps out from behind the couch, and yells, "Boo!"

Gracie darts a startled glance at her brother. Her lips tremble and her mouth puckers. Jay-Son watches her with a confused expression. "Mom, I didn't do anything," he says.

"It's not you, sweetie." I give him a reassuring glance and I lift Gracie into my arms. Her body feels hot. I put my palm on her forehead and realize that she has a fever. She had played with her food during dinner and hardly ate. I pour some apple juice into a plastic mug for her but she pushes it away. Beads of moisture glisten on her brow. I bounce her in my arms, but she's inconsolable.

I am reminded of the time when Jay-Son's appendicitis had flared up, and now my apprehension grows. If only she were old enough to tell me what's wrong with her.

"Jay, please call Dad. Tell him Gracie is sick and I need him to go to the hospital with us."

While he dials Wen-Lung's the number, I wipe Gracie's brow with a wet wash cloth. After a while Jay-Son says, "Dad's not home."

"Try Mrs Liu. Maybe you can stay with her for a few hours while I take Gracie."

I hear him dial the phone again. A few moments later he shakes his head. No one's picking up. It's Saturday evening after all. I glance at my wristwatch. Almost eight. Maybe Keith is home by now. Jay-Son tries him, and he picks up. He's just returned and will come over right away. He shows up in twenty minutes and helps me bundle a thrashing Gracie into her snowsuit and herds us into the elevator and into his car, parked at the front in the driveway. It's a relief to have someone take charge of me, even for a while.

At the hospital we walk through the emergency entrance and Keith drives away to find a parking spot. After a nurse finishes registering us, we sit down in the waiting area and Keith and Jay-Son start playing a game with their hands called Rock Paper Scissors. There's a boy about Jay-Son's age sitting nearby and he sidles closer toward them.

Keith glances up and smiles at the boy. "Would you like to play too?"

The boy's mouth curves tentatively. He turns to look at the door leading to the examination rooms, and then he nods.

"I'm Keith, and this is Jay. What's your name?"

"I'm Patrick." The boy sits down on the chair that Keith pulls up.

Patrick replaces Keith in the game and the two boys wave

their hands, laughing and hooting each time Keith pronounces a winner. I watch the game for a bit. Then Gracie squirms and I get up to pace around the waiting room. Someone brushes past me, his shoulder grazing mine, making me stop. Hostile eyes blaze at me from a scruffy face. The man stops and looks towards Keith, Jay-Son, and Patrick.

"Patrick, what are you doing here? I told you to sit over there and not disturb anyone," the man bellows.

Patrick's head bobs up. He jumps to his feet. Keith smiles at the stranger and says, "He's not disturbing us. In fact, he's good company for our boy here."

Keith's words send a warm glow through me. But it is short-lived. The man casts a disdainful look at us and grabs his son's hand. "Come along. Let's leave this place and all the riffraff here."

Keith's jaws tighten and he clenches his fists. I hold my breath and watch as he uncurls his fists and lifts his chin up a little higher. With a thin smile on his lips, he turns away from the stranger. He ruffles Jay-Son's hair and says, "Now where were we? Let's pretend that the rude man didn't interrupt us."

In India sometimes children in the streets would imitate the Chinese and laugh, chanting "Ching-chong, ching-chong!" The same racist behavior from a grown man in Canada stings much more. But I know I shouldn't let it affect me because for every bigot out there, there are thousands of more decent and open-minded people.

Like most aches and pains that magically disappear after a doctor's ministration, Gracie's fever recedes the next day. The infection in her ear has healed without further incident. Life returns to normal, except now my love for Keith has grown even stronger, if that's possible, and my respect for him doubled.

· 24 ·

"Dad doesn't live with Megan anymore," Jay-Son says as soon as I let him inside. He walks past me into the living room, and I scoop Gracie up. "He lives there." He points to a white apartment building visible from our windows.

"Did you spend the day there?" I'm a little shaken.

Jay-Son nods. "Yup. He lives with two other men in that place."

Questions come racing through my mind. Has Wen-Lung really left Megan? What does this mean for our impending divorce? Who are these people Wen-Lung has moved in with? Can I trust my children to be among them? I'm aware that single Hakka men often share apartments to cut costs. And they often fall into questionable habits.

Gracie squirms. I put her down and watch her toddle away. Trying to sound casual I ask Jay-Son, "What did you do today?"

Jay-Son's face breaks into a smile. "This man who I'm supposed to call Uncle Johnny taught me some magic tricks. You wanna watch, Mom? Can I borrow a quarter from you?"

I give him a quarter and sit down on the sofa. He slaps it against his wrist and covers it with a palm. Then he rubs his forearm, slowly moving the coin higher and higher up. When he lifts his hand the coin has disappeared. I pretend to gape in awe at the vanishing coin which is really hiding between his fingers. "So, do you like this Uncle Johnny?"

"Yeah, he's nice. There's this other man, Uncle Gary, who didn't say much to me. He just sat and watched TV most of the time.

He wouldn't let me watch my shows."

I search my brain wondering who these two men are. We tend to know most Hakka by their Chinese names. Our English names, if we have them, are meant for non-Chinese people.

"And what did Gracie do while you were learning tricks?" I can't dismiss my unease with Wen-Lung's new living arrangement. He has been avoiding me since I asked him to speed up our divorce a few months ago. When he comes to pick up the children he simply buzzes the lobby's intercom. I take them down and he greets me with a grunt and leaves. In the evening he buzzes to announce himself and sends them upstairs on their own.

"She played with Dad. Later he took us to the mall and bought us hot dogs for lunch. When we went back to Dad's apartment, Gracie took a nap."

"And was this Uncle Gary still there when you got back?"

Jay-Son purses his lips. "Yeah, he was still watching TV, so I played with those new cars that Uncle Keith bought."

He waits, then asks, "Mom, are you going to marry Uncle Keith?"

I am speechless for a moment. "Why . . . why do you ask?"

"My friend Sammy's older brother looks at his girlfriend the same way that Uncle Keith looks at you. And you look at him the same way." He grins with a wicked gleam in his eyes.

"Don't be silly," I tell him, blushing.

"How come you didn't marry Uncle Keith if you knew him before you got married to Dad?" He watches me with a smug expression. "Mom, I'm not a little kid anymore. Some of my friends' parents are divorced, and some have remarried. In case you want to give me a new dad, I'll be happy with Uncle Keith."

If Keith were here, he would be delighted to hear this conversation. Clearly whatever he has been doing has worked with Jay-Son. Still, it's one thing for Jay-Son to give me "permission" to marry Keith, and quite something else to find out he's his real father.

◆ ◆ ◆

A few days later, Keith drops by while Joy is working the late shift. Agog with ill-concealed curiosity, Jay-Son asks, "Why is Uncle Keith visiting on a weeknight?"

I rest my hands on his shoulders and gaze into his eyes. "We have to tell you something."

"Are you planning to get married?" Jay-Son asks in a hushed tone.

I pause and search for the right words to come to me. Then I nod and allow myself a quick glance at Keith who, despite his own tension, gives me a reassuring smile. Taking a long breath I say, "Yes, we are. How do you feel about it?"

Jay-Son shrugs. "Mom, I knew this would happen. I'm cool with it."

"There's another thing we want you to know."

Keith invites Jay-Son to sit next to him on the sofa. Then turning to look into his son's eyes he asks, "Do you trust me?"

Jay-Son nods.

"Well, we want you to know that we both love you very much. Before you were born, your mom and I were in love and because of that we made a baby together."

Jay-Son's eyes grow round and luminous. I kneel down in front of him and hold both his hands. "Jay-Son, honey, you are Uncle Keith's son. We made you together before I was married."

"Uncle Keith is not my uncle? He's my dad?" Jay-Son's voice quivers.

Keith drapes one arm over Jay-Son's shoulders. "Yes, are you okay with that?"

"What about my other dad? I mean is he . . . "

Keith says gently, "Jay, you are my son because your mom and I made you together. That doesn't mean your other dad is no longer your father. He raised you, and he loves you too."

Jay-Son knits his eyebrows together. "So now I have two dads? I don't think Dad's going to like that."

Keith and I exchange a glance. He rumples Jay-Son's hair. "Don't worry about that. It'll all work out."

I wonder how. Rising slowly from the floor I give Jay-Son's hands another gentle squeeze. "Can we keep this our secret for now?"

"Okay, but I'm telling you Dad's not going to be happy about sharing me with Uncle Keith."

"I like you, Uncle Keith, but . . . " Jay-Son's eyes glisten and his lips tremble. Then inexplicably he dashes out and the next thing I hear is his bedroom door banging shut. I rush after him, filled with dread and concern. As I knock on Jay-Son's door Keith hovers behind me. Our eyes meet and I shake my head to let him know that he should stay out.

Entering the room I notice Jay-Son lying face down on his bed. "Jay, honey," I say quietly, "do you want to talk about it?"

Jay-Son says in a muffled tone, "Leave me alone. I don't want to talk." He turns sideways. "Why is my dad not my dad anymore and Uncle Keith is suddenly my dad?"

"Oh, sweetie," I say as I sit on the edge of the bed, "I'm so sorry to confuse you like this. Uncle Keith never knew about you until recently."

"Then why aren't you married to him instead of Dad?"

How long have I chided myself with the same question. Out loud I say, "Sometimes adults do things that seem strange. There's usually a good reason for what we do. You will understand that eventually. One thing is certain, both Uncle Keith and I adore you."

Jay-Son pushes himself up on the bed. Hugging his knees he says, "Er . . . do I have to call Uncle Keith dad too? Do I still have to visit my other dad? I don't like his new place. I can't do anything there, and Uncle Gary won't let me watch TV."

"If you're more comfortable calling him Uncle Keith, then that's fine. Maybe when you get used to the idea, you can start to call him Dad."

That's a relief, I say to myself.

Now how do we break the news to Wen-Lung.

Jay-Son interrupts my thoughts. "So, can I stay home on Saturday? I don't want to go to Dad's apartment."

"Uh . . . maybe."

◆ ◆ ◆

Wen-Lung curses. He yells. He threatens. Every explctive is a promise to make my life miserable. "You conniving bitch. You slept with another man before we got married. How do I know you didn't do the same again after I came here? How many more men were there?"

I flinch and glance around the coffee shop at the other tables, all occupied. No one seems to be noticing the drama between us or else they are discreetly looking away. Taking a deep breath I tell myself to stay calm. "Keith was the only one, and only because I was in love with him, and it was before our marriage."

"So you're not as pure as you'd like people to think. Our goody-goody Maylei with her dirty little secret."

I had thought that the best place to have this conversation was somewhere public, where Wen-Lung would be forced to rein in his emotions. I was wrong. "What I did doesn't come close to what you did. You cheated on me while we were married and had a baby with Megan. Then you cheated on me again after Gracie was born."

"So you've decided to marry the father of your bastard after all these years?" Wen-Lung's mouth curls into a sneer. "Who is he? Do I know him?"

I cringe but stay calm. "You don't know him."

"I've been hearing a rumor that a half-brained man has been

visiting you. Is he your boyfriend?"

Do not rise to his bait. It doesn't matter what derogatory remarks he makes about Keith, just ignore him. He's forgetting that his own son with Megan is also of mixed blood, half-brained, as he says.

"My friends come in different colors. I don't have to justify anyone to you."

"I don't want an Anglo-Indian twit raising my kids."

I stare at him like I want to murder him right there. But I push my chair back. "Jay-Son isn't your son, and I will be friends with whoever I choose."

"You can't leave yet. We're not finished."

"I'm done listening to your insults."

"Don't go yet." He lowers his voice, sounding almost conciliatory. "Are you going to marry him?"

"It's none of your business."

"If you keep your boyfriend away, I'll come by and help you sometimes."

"Why would I want that?"

"I still want to be part of my children's lives."

"You can continue to see them."

His expression softens. He points to the chair. "Please sit down, Maylei. Let's be adults about this. I want to come back and raise the kids with you. I still love Jay-Son. He was my son before you told me all this . . . this . . . ."

I lower myself down on the edge of the seat. Even if he means it, he's not being realistic. "Wen-Lung, we are way past that. You know that too, and you know also we will never be able to get past what we've both done. Let's move on with our lives."

Wen-Lung narrows his eyes and compresses his lips. "Well, we're not divorced yet. I don't want that half-brained boyfriend of yours raising my daughter."

I scrape my chair back and stand up to go.

He pushes himself up with his palms on the table and leans across inches from my face, scowling. "If I find out that you're seeing this Anglo-Indian, I will not make it easy for you."

"What will you do? You can't do anything to stop our divorce."

"Maybe I can't stop your leaving the marriage, but I can certainly make your life difficult if I want to." A sinister smile follows. "You know that the Hakka community will never accept you again if you marry an Anglo-Indian. I will make sure of that."

"It's nobody's business who I marry. And since I'm already on the outside now as a divorcee, why should I care anymore about what they think?"

· 25 ·

Keith's sister Astrid and his father, my former boss, Mr Wilson, arrive in Toronto on the last Friday of June. Their timing couldn't be more perfect. Jay-Son is starting to get used to the idea of Keith as a father and his outbursts are now far and few. His summer vacation has just begun, and my boss graciously lets me take a week off from work.

The next day Keith brings Astrid and Mr Wilson to the apartment. It's been three years since our last meeting. So much has happened during the intervening time. They are now reappearing in my life as my future in-laws. As soon as Astrid catches sight of me, she runs and almost stumbles into my open arms. The three years have added a few more pounds on her frame.

"Maylei, you look lovely. I am so happy for you and Keith. And where is my handsome nephew?"

I call to Jay-Son to come outside while Gracie peers from behind my legs. Astrid bends forward to speak to her. "Oh, you must be Grace, you darling little thing. You're cute as a button."

Mr Wilson lumbers toward me. "Maylei, you are such a welcome sight. Let me take a good look at my future daughter-in-law." I extend my hand out, but he pulls me and Gracie into a bear hug.

I have never seen Mr Wilson this emotional before. When I worked for him, there had always been an unspoken employer-employee barrier. Now with one embrace that invisible wall crumbles, and he is family. Jay-Son appears at the end of the hallway, looking into the living room, eyes darting from one face to another. He tries to look indifferent to all the excitement, but the sparkle in his eyes speaks volumes. Although I had prepared him for this meeting, anxiety clutches my chest into a tight squeeze. I watch anxiously as Astrid approaches Jay-Son with a more measured gait before flinging her arms around his neck. While she showers him with kisses on his cheeks, his body stiffens, and his mouth twitches in a tremulous smile.

Oblivious to his discomfort, Astrid drags him to meet her father. Mr Wilson stands back to gaze at his grandson as if memorizing every detail of his face. I quell the tears welling up behind my eyelids. I feel Keith's hand reaching for mine from behind and squeezing it.

I turn to say something to Keith, and that's when I notice Joy talking to a stranger, who's standing at the door. In the excitement of our meeting, I didn't see the newcomer, stocky and a couple of inches taller than Joy.

Keith calls out, "Hey Mike, I see you've met Joy. This is Maylei." Turning to me he says, "My cousin Mike also flew in with Dad and Astrid. He's my dad's nephew, Nevil's younger brother."

He saunters off to join Jay-Son, who is fidgeting with the TV converter on the couch.

Mike says, "I've heard a lot about you, Maylei."

"Nothing bad, I hope. So, is this also your first trip to Canada?"

Mike smiles, his cheeks dimpling like a school boy's. "Yes, I've never been out of India before. This is a new experience for me."

Joy, looking flushed and sounding breathless, says, "Mike is planning to stay for four months."

I arch an eyebrow at her. She turns red. I turn to Mike. The spark between the two is hard to ignore. How unusual for Joy, who has never displayed any emotions toward men like this before. She carries her singlehood with pride and without apology. She received many marriage proposals from eligible bachelors from the Hakka community, but she insisted that she would marry only for love. Now the offers have stopped. Her status in Canada hasn't motivated her to find a husband who can offer her permanent residency.

As I serve drinks and snacks, a general sense of contentment settling in the room, a feeling of utter happiness engulfs me; I want to stretch the afternoon for as long as possible. No doubt a time will come when I will need to draw upon this memory to help me over life's hurdles. For now I'm content with this blissful moment.

◆ ◆ ◆

On Sunday after lunch, Keith and his family drop by again. Astrid insists that she and I go out for coffee, leaving the others behind in my apartment. We amble along the sidewalk in the summer heat. I squint my eyes behind my shades at the hazy sunshine bouncing off the passing vehicles. Although she is acclimatized to the sweltering humidity of Calcutta, Astrid has trouble walking in this Toronto heat. I slow down and she slides an arm into my elbow.

"I've never seen Keith so happy before."

"I am so fortunate to have him."

"My brother is a good man. I can't bear to see Keith suffer again."

I hear the gentle warning in her tone. Although taken aback at first, I understand where she's coming from.

"You never have to fear that I will do anything to hurt Keith. I have no intention of letting him go or letting anything come between us."

Astrid's arm tightens around mine. We walk in compatible silence until we arrive at a coffee shop a few minutes later. Standing at the door I scan the faces of the Sunday afternoon crowd for any familiar face I may want to avoid. I don't wish to bump into Wen-Lung or any of his friends. Satisfied that they are not lurking among these coffee drinkers, I search for a pair of seats. Spotting a small table in a quiet space by the window overlooking Bloor Street, I lead Astrid there and ask her to take a seat while I get our brew.

When I return, Astrid asks, "When are you and Keith planning to get married?"

"My lawyer tells me that my divorce will be finalized later this year. We won't plan the wedding until that happens."

Astrid stares at me with unnerving intensity, her brown eyes reminding me so much of her brother. "Have you ever considered moving in together?"

My jaws slacken and my mouth gapes at Astrid. She never ceases to astonish me. All my life I've believed that North Americans and Europeans are unapologetic about premarital living arrangements, while we Asians are different, or so I think. Yet, here is this woman—straight out of the puritanical social landscape of Calcutta—suggesting that I live in sin with her brother. Yes, I have considered it, but only in the privacy of my own thoughts.

Cautiously, I ask, "What will your parents think? Where we come from people still frown on stuff like this, remember?"

She makes a dismissive gesture with her hand. "Offo . . . don't be such a prude."

I give a quick laugh. "Actually, Keith and I did discuss it not too long ago, but I asked him to wait until after your visit. But, what about your parents? I can't imagine them approving this step."

"They'll get over it. They only want what's best for Keith, and right now, they know you're it. And my dad is so proud of the way his son has taken over the responsibility of being a father to Jay-Son. Just look at how both your children are completely taken up with Keith. They seem to adore him."

"The three of them are my life. I can't imagine what it would be like to live without them."

· 26 ·

Astrid and Mr Wilson stayed four weeks and left. Soon after, I followed up on my decision and moved in with Keith. Nevil and Leslie had already moved into their own house. And Mike moved in with Joy.

It's after ten and my eyelids begin to droop. Keith pats my arm and says gently, "Let's go to bed. You've had a long day."

"Uh . . . okay." I stretch and yawn.

The phone rings. Keith picks it up after two rings. "Oh, hello Joy," he says after a short pause.

It's rather late for Joy to call. I turn a questioning gaze at Keith. He puts up a hand to tell me to wait and listens as Joy finishes. Then he turns to look at me with a concerned look.

"What's wrong?" I ask, anxiously.

"When did this happen?" he says into the mouthpiece.

Silence, and then, "Where is he now?"

Another silence. "Okay, I'll come by right away."

Keith hangs up the phone, the furrows on his brow even deeper. "Mike is in jail. He was arrested with a few other illegal immigrants at the restaurant where he works. Joy thinks that someone squealed to the officials."

"Oh no, not now! Not when they're about to get married."

Joy has already received her immigration documents, and she and Mike plan to be married next weekend.

Keith grabs his car keys off the hook on the closet door. "I'm going to pick up Joy right now. We'll meet her lawyer at the police station."

"Give her my love. Tell her not to panic."

Keith is gone for several hours. I don't hear from him until he tiptoes into our bedroom after midnight. "What happened?" I ask, and switch on the night lamp on the bedside table. Unbuttoning his shirt, he says, "I think everything will turn out fine. Alan Silver was already at the police station when Joy and I arrived. He got Mike out, but there's a lot of paperwork involved."

"But why did the police raid this particular restaurant?"

Keith stares at me with troubled eyes. "This may sound crazy, but Joy believes that Wen-Lung was behind it. He tipped the immigration department about the illegals working at that place."

My hand covers my mouth in disbelief. "Does Joy know for sure?"

"No one can be sure except Wen-Lung. Joy says that he worked at the restaurant after he got fired from his previous job—"

"Wen-Lung got fired from his job? I didn't know that."

"That's what happened. Then he got fired again after working at this particular restaurant for just a few weeks. Mike says that Wen-Lung was caught stealing from the cash register. He did it more than once."

I cannot comprehend why Wen-Lung would do such a thing. This cannot be the same person I married in Calcutta. "It looks like something's not quite right with Wen-Lung. The friends he hangs out with aren't the kind to help him."

"What's wrong with his friends?"

"They are all on welfare, they rent a government-subsidized apartment, and who knows what they do with all the time they have."

◆ ◆ ◆

A week later, Joy and Mike stand before the judge while Nevil, Leslie, Keith, Jay-Son, Gracie and I look on. The ceremony is simple, almost clinical, until the judge says, "You may now kiss the bride."

But a deep unease mars my enjoyment of the wedding celebrations. I may not have seen or heard from Wen-Lung for some time, but his presence hovers over me like a dark cloud. There's a sense of impending doom sitting on my shoulders waiting to pounce when I least expect it.

27

The four of us head down to the island ferry dock at Harbourfront in Keith's car. At the terminal there are lines snaking from the ticket gates to almost the sidewalk. I fan my face with a glossy ad that someone stuck into my hand a few minutes ago. Every now and then we shuffle forward, Keith pushing Gracie in a light-weight stroller while Jay-Son makes faces at her.

"How do you manage to stay so cool in this heat?" I huff at Keith.

He flashes me a smile underneath his Toronto Blue Jays' cap. "Easy, don't stress about it."

I whack his arm with my makeshift fan. "Try not to break a sweat telling me that."

"Hey, Dad, over here, Dad," Jay-Son yells.

My heart sinks. Dad can only mean one person: Jay-Son still calls Keith "uncle." Although the two have developed a close bond, in his mind, Wen-Lung is still his father. With a feeling of dread I turn around and stare straight into Wen-Lung's eyes. A family of three stands between us. An odd expression crosses his gaunt face, much thinner than I remember it. His gaze falls on Gracie and I wonder what he thinks. Although he hasn't made any attempt to connect with us in over a year, he is never far from my thoughts. His continued stalling has put my wedding plans on hold longer than I hoped.

Keith saunters down the line, sticks out his hand and says, "Hi Wen-Lung, what a coincidence. I'm glad to finally meet you."

Wen-Lung stares at Keith with a sullen face. He mutters, "Oh, sure . . . it wasn't my idea to come here today. Just look at this crowd." His hand grazes Keith's palm, and his eyes sweep over the masses with ill-concealed contempt.

I glance at the little boy standing quietly by his side. "Is it just the two of you?" I ask, trying to sound normal.

"Yes, Megan wanted to treat herself to a day out with her friends. So I brought Ryan to Centre Island because she promised him I would."

Wen-Lung's presence casts a gloom over our otherwise sunny and cloudless day. Oblivious to my anxiety, Jay-Son says, "Dad, stay with us. We're going to have a picnic there."

A smile comes over Wen-Lung's face and he looks from me to Jay-Son and then to Keith. "Maybe I will," he says softly.

If it weren't for the sunglasses shielding my eyes, my fury would have been exposed for everyone to see. "Okay with me. We've got plenty of food." My voice sounds half-choked even to my own ears.

Keith squeezes my shoulder. "Yes, please do join us."

"Gee, thanks. That's very nice of you to invite us to share your lunch."

I ignore the sarcasm and shrug with feigned nonchalance. "You're welcome."

At the ticket booth, Keith pays for the four of us and we wait for Wen-Lung and Ryan on the other side of the gate. Together we shuffle up the ramp and enter the ferry. Jay-Son runs upstairs to the middle deck, and Ryan follows him. Keith and I lift Gracie in her stroller and go up the stairs to where Jay-Son and Ryan are standing behind the wire barrier at the front, waving at the passing boats. Watching them I can almost ignore Wen-Lung's dampening effect on us.

I look around and can't see him. Finally, there he is, sitting on a bench mid-ship, shoulders hunched, elbows on his knees. Unaware that I'm watching him, he looks vulnerable and sad.

I don't hate this man, the father of our daughter. I had married Wen-Lung with high hopes that we would remain compatible and grow old together because that is the Hakka way in Tangra. Yet here we are, farther apart than anything physical can bridge.

The sound of Keith's voice brings me back to the present. He passes the stroller to me and joins the boys. Leaning over Jay-Son from behind, he points to a boat filled with rowers dipping and raising their oars. He whispers something in his son's ear. Jay-Son turns. Grinning, he lifts his hand and the two bump fists, sharing a moment that excludes all of us.

My heart swells with love for the two. I find myself wondering if what I'd hoped for with Keith eleven years ago would have ended up as we are today. Would we have stayed in love, weathered the hardships of immigration?

The ferry starts to move away from the dock. Jay-Son and Ryan yell together, "Yeah . . . we're sailing."

Soon we arrive on the other shore and the ferry docks. People begin to stream out. Keith lifts the stroller and we walk down the steps, herding the children ahead of us. Wen-Lung takes his time to follow at the back.

As soon as we step on the walkway by the lake, Jay-Son turns to me with shining eyes. "Mom, can we go to the rides first? I want to go on a roller-coaster."

"Okay, you lead the way."

With a child's nose for direction when it matters to him, Jay-Son gets us to Centreville in no time. At the main ticket kiosk where we line up to buy tickets for the rides, I scan around for Wen-Lung. I don't see him anywhere. "Keith, have you seen Wen-Lung?" For an inexplicable reason, I am worried.

"The last time I saw him he had stopped to tie his shoelaces. He knows we're coming here first, so I'm sure he'll catch up."

Keith pays for the tickets. He follows Jay-Son to the entrance for the log flume ride.

Jay-Son calls out, "Ryan, come on up."

But Ryan hangs back, his lips quivering, tears brimming to the edge of his eyelids. "What's the matter? Don't you want to ride with Jay and Uncle Keith?" I ask.

He shakes his head. "Where's my dad?"

I wish Wen-Lung would hurry up and join us. The thought of facing a tantrum from a child I barely know fills me with dread. "Come, Ryan, stay close to me. We'll find another ride for you next." I smile to reassure him. He sidles closer to me while I signal Keith and Jay-Son to keep going.

Gracie says, "Gracie wants ride too." She points to the log flume.

"No, not this one," I tell her. "We'll go to the merry-go-round. Would you like that?"

She agrees. I glance around . . . still no sign of Wen-Lung. We wave at Keith and Jay-Son when their log reaches the top. They raise their hands and in seconds they slosh down, water splashing around them.

A short while later, Jay-Son comes running to me. "Hey, Mom, can we do it again?"

"Later, sweetie. Let's go on the merry-go-round." I point to the carousel where the antique animals bounce with jaunty grace on a circular path.

"I want to sit on a horse," Ryan says.

Jay-Son takes Ryan's hand and they run off together. Every now and then while we wait for our turn I scan the area around us hoping for a glimpse of Wen-Lung. Where could he have disappeared to? How inconsiderate and irresponsible of him to leave his son with us without saying a word.

The carousel halts, and we shuffle inside the gate, leaving Keith outside to take pictures. Ryan picks a gray horse and Jay-Son climbs up a prancing golden-brown stallion. I put Gracie on a rabbit and stand beside her.

When the music starts, the animals begin to rise and fall and the carousel turns. We wave to Keith each time we pass him. At the end of the ride, I glance around once again hoping to see Wen-Lung.

When the ride is over, I go up to Keith. "I can't believe Wen-Lung would ditch Ryan like this and disappear," I mutter.

Keith frowns. "That's really odd."

"Do you think maybe he can't find us?"

"I'm positive he saw us heading this way when he stopped to tie his shoelaces. He even waved at me to keep going."

My hand gets tugged. I look down and Ryan lisps, "Wasn't that fun? Let's go on another ride."

I tell him, "Okay, let's ride those floating white swans."

Keith says, "Maylei, you ride with the kids while I try to find Wen-Lung."

Gracie and I hop on one boat and Jay-Son and Ryan ride another. Gracie's excitement infects us all as she squeals at the boys when they call out to her. All too soon we are back, and the boys call out for food.

Keith comes striding over, shaking his head. He's not found Wen-Lung.

"Okay, lunch," I say to the boys, and we start to walk away from Centreville.

"We can set up our base there." Keith points to a grassy knoll straight ahead. A bridge on the left spans a body of water.

As we trudge up toward a picnic table, a large crowd by the water draws our attention. Keith says, "I wonder what's going on there. Maylei, go ahead and set up for lunch. I'll check it out and be right back." He jogs away.

I spread a bedsheet on the grass and cover the wooden table with a vinyl table cloth. Jay-Son helps me unpack the food and utensils. I serve meatball curry, salad, and bread to Jay-Son and Ryan. Gracie says, "No curry." I hand her a hot dog. Ryan eyes it and says, "Can I get a hot dog too?"

"Sure, Ryan. Would you like to try a little bit of curry? It's not spicy."

"No," he says vehemently, and then bites into his hot dog. Looking up, I see Keith talking to a man in a white T-shirt, who's pointing at the water. After a long pause, Keith nods at the man and eases through the crowd toward the water's edge. A short while later, he jogs back to us. One glance at his face sends my heart lurching.

"It's Wen-Lung," he says grimly.

"What happened?" A strangled whisper escapes my mouth.

"He was seen walking into the water. One minute he was standing, and then the next, gone. They pulled him out. The paramedics are on the way."

28

Wen-Lung's suicide attempt has left me on edge, expecting a storm to unleash its wrath on our lives. If he had worn a banner on his head announcing his depression, I still wouldn't have thought he'd resort to ending his life. This time there was a large audience watching, but next time he might do the deed without anyone's knowledge. I'm certain of one thing; he is willing to do anything desperate to draw attention to himself. If only he would seek professional help, but Hakka men seem united in their disdain for mental-health counselling.

That day I accompanied him to the hospital in the ambulance. He had said earlier that he barely spoke to Megan now, making contact only when she wanted him to do something. The same could be said about his relationship with me. But guilt burns in me like a flame I can't douse. Obviously, seeing Keith with me and the children, and how happy we were, had driven him to the brink.

Wen-Lung was conscious when the paramedics loaded him to their vehicle. He looked vulnerable and tugged at my heart-strings. This was someone I had pledged, at one time, to be my partner for life. On an impulse I clasped his hand in mine.

He whispered, "Maylei, please come back to me. I'm sorry about what I did. We could be a family again."

I slowly pulled my hand back and shook my head. "Don't talk. You need to rest."

He closed his eyes and drifted off. When we arrived at the hospital, I waited until a doctor came out and told me that he would recover fully. I informed the doctor that we were separated and left, and did not return again. He was in capable hands, and I did not want to lead him on with hopes of a reunion.

That was two weeks ago. He hasn't tried to contact us since then.

"What's the matter?" Keith asks, standing behind me. His hands drop on my shoulders and he begins to knead my muscles.

"I was thinking about what happened the other day at Centre Island."

"Why am I not surprised?" Keith's fingers move down my back, pressing and loosening the knots.

"I can't help wondering if he'll try something drastic again."

"If he doesn't value his life that much, then let him do what he wants to do. You can't stop him." Keith purses his lips into a hard line.

"Wen-Lung doesn't mean anything to me now—but we're connected by our common history and previous marriage. I'm thinking about the children. It would be awful for them if he makes another suicide attempt. Jay-Son's already traumatized by what happened. He can't help thinking of Wen-Lung as his father. It will take time."

"That man is unstable and you should never allow him to be alone with the kids ever."

"What if he wants to see Gracie?" How peaceful our lives were when Wen-Lung stopped seeing the children. All communication with him had been through the lawyers.

"Then we'll have to make sure that he's never alone with Gracie."

◆ ◆ ◆

Wen-Lung starts calling me once a week, sometimes more. He calls to speak to the daughter he's ignored for over a year. Gracie shows no interest in talking to him. She listens for a few seconds and then hands the phone back to me. "Mama, you talk," she says.

"Maylei, I want to take Gracie out every Saturday," Wen-Lung says to me.

"You know what a handful Gracie can be. You've never taken care of a three-year old by yourself. And I'm worried that your place isn't child-proofed. Let's not be too hasty right now."

He hangs up in a huff.

The following Saturday, he calls again while I'm home by myself. "Have you decided what to do about Gracie yet, Maylei?"

I suppress a sigh. "I'm not sure that I want you taking her to your apartment. I don't know where you're staying and who your roommates are."

"So you don't trust me with her?"

"It's not that I don't trust you. If you want to visit with her, then let's arrange to meet somewhere she'll be comfortable." I wish there was some way I could dissuade him but I can't deny him his parental rights.

"We'll see."

I wonder now what he will do. Moments later, the phone rings again. I expect it to be Keith, he's taken the children to the mall to shop for Halloween costumes.

I pick up the phone.

"Is this Maylei?" a male Hakka voice asks.

"Yes, who is this?"

"I'm a friend of your husband. People call me Rocky."

I resist the urge to correct the caller about my marital status. "Why are you calling me?"

"Wen-Lung owes me money and I need to be paid back."

My breath catches. I cannot think for some moments. Then angrily, I say, "He's no longer my husband. We're about to be divorced."

"But you're still his wife legally. Someone has to pay his gambling debt."

"Gambling debt?"

"Yes, and don't tell me you don't know he plays poker. He's not a smart player. He loses more than he wins."

"How much does he owe you?" I ask and then instantly regret the question.

"A few thousand dollars and counting. He likes to drown his sorrows in his cards."

Something snaps in my head. "Well, you can't call yourself his friend if you let him play like this. I don't have that kind of money, and as I said, we're no longer married."

"Somebody has to pay up," he growls.

Anger and fear keep me going. "Why don't you get the money from Wen-Lung? He's the one who's in debt to you."

"I would if I could. He says that between paying you and the other bitch, he's broke."

Wen-Lung hasn't given me a dime in months, but it's irrelevant to this man. "That still doesn't make me responsible for his debt."

"Ha. Don't be so sure."

"Goodbye, Mister." With a trembling finger I end the call. Then I release the button and furiously dial Wen-Lung's number.

Three rings later, "Hello."

"Wen-Lung, what are you thinking, gambling with so much money?"

"I don't know what you're talking about."

"Really? Who the heck is Rocky then?"

"Oh. Don't worry about him. I know what I'm doing. I'll win it all back, just wait and see."

My knuckles tense around the phone and I take a deep breath. "Don't you see what you're doing? Instead of gambling more, you should start repaying your debt."

"You have no idea what's going on. I've had a streak of bad luck, that's all. It will pass and then I'll start to win again, just like I did before."

"How long has this been going on?"

"It's all your fault, Maylei. You drove me out of my own home. When I first started to play, it was to kill time and we played for nickels and quarters."

"You're a grown man, Wen-Lung. Nobody forced you to gamble."

"What would you have me do? Two ex-wives who only want my money. I had to come up with a way to make more."

"First of all, don't use the same brush to paint Megan and me. I've cut you more breaks on your child support payments than you deserve. If you have time on your hands, maybe you should find another job to help make ends meet instead of gambling."

"I don't have to listen to you. Just leave me alone. I'll find a way to pay my debts."

"Well then, you tell your friend Rocky to stop bothering me. Your debt is not my concern."

When I hang up the phone, a mixture of indignation and unease simmer in my head. I never expected Wen-Lung to gamble. While we were together, he didn't know how to play poker. I don't know him anymore. He did live in Canada for five years on his own. That could change a man.

I raise my eyes to look out the kitchen window when I hear the sound of car doors slamming. Keith and the children have returned.

"What's wrong, babe? You look flustered," Keith says as soon as he sees me. He pecks my cheek and slides his windbreaker off. "Did something happen?"

I glance around to make sure the kids are gone. "Wen-Lung's been gambling for high stakes, and he's in trouble." I tell Keith about the call from Rocky and my conversation with Wen-Lung.

Keith clenches his teeth. "You're not paying Wen-Lung's debts for him. He dug the hole . . . let him climb out of it himself."

I don't know what comes over me. For the second time

this afternoon, something snaps in my head. "Easy for you to say. Wen-Lung is still my husband on paper. We're not legally divorced, remember?"

His eyes soften and he says, "I didn't mean to sound so callous, but I don't want you to get hurt. You are not responsible for Wen-Lung."

"That man . . . that Rocky, or whoever he is, threatened to do something bad if I don't pay up. He didn't have to spell it out; he implied it."

"I think Rocky didn't say what he would do because he thinks a vague threat will be enough to frighten you into paying."

"Maybe you're right." I desperately want to believe him.

· 29 ·

As Keith predicted, Rocky's threat did not materialize and my divorce went through despite Wen-Lung's delay tactics. But being divorced from Wen-Lung doesn't mean that he's no longer part of our lives. He is Gracie's father and his visits are turning into contentious battles with her. Of course, his suicide attempt and mental stability are never far from my mind. When I confided in Joy she offered her apartment as a meeting place where father and daughter could spend Saturday afternoons together.

I try to make the visits pleasant, but the girl is starting to show her own mind. When I drop her off with Joy to wait for her father, she throws a temper tantrum. I feel torn seeing her sob as she writhes out of Joy's restraining arms to follow me. Sometimes I hang around when Gracie seems more difficult than usual. It isn't unusual for me to bring a book and read in Joy's bedroom for the entire afternoon when Wen-Lung visits with Gracie in case she becomes uncontrollable. On days when she's her cheerful self, Wen-Lung takes her to the mall. While I worried the first time this happened, when he brought her back calm and happy, my mind rested and became more accepting of these little trips.

◆ ◆ ◆

On Christmas Day, we gather around our tree. Jay-Son and Gracie fix their shining eyes on the candy canes hooked over the branches and the colorful gift-wrapped boxes—presents that Nevil and Leslie, and Mike and Joy have just piled below the tree.

The children already opened their presents from Santa Claus earlier this morning—new clothes which they tossed aside when they saw their new toys. Keith and I decided to splurge and buy a Nintendo game console for Jay-Son. For Gracie we bought an inflatable Popples Playhouse that she could wiggle into and pop her head out of a hole, also a stuffed puppy that she immediately christened Bonnie.

Hugging Bonnie with one arm, Gracie sidles up to her Aunt Joy. "Look what Santa brought for me."

Joy beams at her and says, "You must have been a good girl for Santa to bring you presents." ·

Gracie nods and her eyes follow Joy's hand, which is picking up a box wrapped in glossy red paper and tied with a green ribbon. "And here's another present for my favorite niece."

It's a Barbie doll.

I serve roast turkey and stuffing, Leslie brought a beef curry, and Joy brought Chinese pastries for dessert. Looking at the table laden with dishes reflecting our Chinese, Anglo-Indian, and now Canadian cultures, I am overcome with a deep sense of gratitude. Unlike me, my children will surely grow up in a kinder and more tolerant world.

My gaze wanders from one happy face to another. Gracie, beside me in her booster chair, shoves a big piece of turkey into her mouth. Leslie sips from a wine glass as she leans back against Nevil's arm draped over the high-back chair. Keith at the opposite end of the table looks flushed with wine and love while Jay-Son, next to him, gobbles everything in sight. Mike coaxes Joy to eat some salad, her stomach revolting at the rich food in front of her. She's expecting.

Keith catches my eye and lifts up his wine glass. "Cheers, everyone, and Merry Christmas to all of you."

We lift our glasses and repeat the sentiment.

◆ ◆ ◆

Later that night, after I've snuggled against Keith, spoon fashion, we whisper intoxicated endearments and how glad we are that all looks well, when the phone rings.

I groan, "Who could be calling at this time of the night?"

Midnight calls do not bring good news.

Keith climbs out of the bed. "I'll get it."

I follow him into the kitchen. He flicks the light switch on, crosses the floor in two big strides, and picks up the receiver. After the initial hello, he hands it to me. "It's your sister."

My heart sinks like lead. Jinlei wouldn't call unless she has urgent news. Calls from Calcutta cost too much.

"Jinlei, how are you?"

"Maylei, I hope I didn't wake you up from your sleep." She sounds disembodied.

"I wasn't asleep."

A pause. "Well . . . there's no easy way to tell you."

My blood rushes to my head. "It's Ma, isn't it?"

"Yes, she's very sick. The doctor says she doesn't have much time left. The cancer is spreading fast."

"When did this happen?" I ask a silly question. "I thought it was gone."

"I don't know. She's been hiding her pain. A few days ago Pa found her doubled up in bed. He took her to the doctor and that's how we found out."

"Where is she now?"

"She's home. The doctor told us to make her comfortable and that's all we can do."

"Oh, Jinlei." Tears stream down my cheeks. I remember my mother when I left India—healthy and bustling with energy, fingers deftly stuffing and folding dumplings. "Is she in a lot of pain?"

"Most of the time she's drugged and asleep. Thank goodness for that."

"I will come home to see her." I choke, wondering if I will get there on time. Nothing can keep me from seeing my mother.

"Please come quickly."

I hang up the phone, stand still for a moment, my palms over my face, and let grief soak through me. I start to sink down to the floor, but Keith wraps me in his arms. Caressing my hair, he asks, "Is it your mom?"

I can't find my voice and nod.

"You must go and be with her."

I nod again.

"Trust me to take good care of the kids."

I bury my face in his chest again and sob. My heart aches for my mother, just turned sixty and unlikely to experience another Lunar New Year which is coming up in a few weeks.

Mother's hand, the skin loose and wrinkled, rests lightly inside mine. Her eyes, sunk into deep receptacles, mirror unimaginable pain as they gaze at my face as though memorizing every detail. I lace my fingers with hers, holding her hand the way she used to hold mine when I was little. Back then, when I followed her to the market square in the morning, her calloused palm would rub my tender flesh like sandpaper. But they communicated to me her love and my sense of belonging to her. Now those same callouses remind me of the hard life she has led.

Sitting by her bedside, a cotton duvet—the bright green, pink and red stripes cheerfully incongruous—upon her, I can only hope that my touch brings her some comfort the way hers used to bring me. I watch her with an aching heart. She lived her entire married life for her family. We will survive her and forever feel bereft. I wish I could do something for her. Make her more comfortable, more happy.

Nostalgia and sadness run deep in my soul, but I also can't ignore now the revulsion at the dirt and grime on the streets. My flight landed mid-afternoon, and our neighbor, Mr Lee, sent his driver in the Ambassador along with my youngest brother, Kam, to pick me up at the airport. I'm glad that I remembered to buy a bottle of Scotch whisky at the duty-free for Mr Lee. Such a small token of appreciation for all the favors he has showered upon us.

The familiar smell of open sewage—a cesspool of leather-tanning chemicals and household waste combined into a thick sludge—cling to my nostrils as I arrive. Soon I won't even notice it once my senses reacquaint with the environment I had called home for over twenty-seven years.

Mother says something I cannot hear. I lean closer to her. In a raspy whisper, she says, "Maylei, I'm so happy you are home. I wanted to see you one more time before I go."

"Of course, I'm here, Ma. I want you to get stronger so we can have long talks and I can tell you all about my life in Canada." I force a lightness into my voice, knowing full well that she will never recover. My only wish is that she will experience a few pain-free days.

"Just seeing you is enough for me. I can now go in peace. If only I could see my grandchildren too." Her words stumble out between labored breaths.

"Jay-Son misses you, his favorite ah-poh. He's got school right now, and we can't afford to fly the whole family here."

"Do you have pictures of them?" Another hoarse whisper.

"Yes." I pick up my purse from the floor and retrieve the envelope containing photos of the children and Keith. I place them in her hands one at a time.

As she slowly stacks one picture on top of another, she asks me a few questions about them. I describe the moments when each snapshot was taken. The pained look in her eyes seem to recede somewhat as the corners of her mouth lift every now and then when I tell her about the mischief Jay-Son and Gracie got into. Then with a sigh she drops the pictures on her lap and closes her eyes. I fear I have tired her out and carefully pry the photos from her slack fingers.

"Maylei, come, let's go to the next room and let your mother rest," Father says softly from the entrance.

I turn around. I did not see him enter. His black hair used to be threaded with gray before I left Tangra four and a half years ago. Now, strands of black thread the white hair. He looks every inch his sixty-three years, and maybe even a few more. This was a man who neighbors would jokingly say was like my older brother. Clutching my purse under one arm and still holding my pictures in my other hand, I follow Father next door to the front room, from where we can view Tangra's main thoroughfare. Hands clasped behind him, he paces soundlessly on bare feet. In my haste to see Mama, I did not notice the reserved—almost chilly—reception I had received from him when I walked in through the front door about an hour ago.

"Pa, are you all right?"

He grunts and walks away from me. When he arrives at the threshold, he turns around to face me, arms crossed. I throw him a questioning glance.

"So, you're planning to marry Keith."

Jinlei warned me in one of her letters that Father couldn't reconcile with my decision to marry someone he disapproves. He came to terms with my decision to separate and divorce Wen-Lung only after Jinlei and my brothers told him about Wen-Lung's infidelity and the child he has fathered with Megan.

"Yes, Papa. Keith is a good man and he's waited many years for me. He wants to raise my children with me." I had written to my parents about Keith and Jay-Son's relationship soon after I revealed it to Wen-Lung. Regardless, had I not done so, the entire community would still have found out.

Father's eyes probe mine with a long stare. Unflinching, I take in the dark bags above the high cheekbones where the lines travel down his cheeks. At last he blinks and asks, "Are you in love with him?"

"I love him so much, it hurts, Papa. If you and Mama had agreed all those years ago, I would have married him instead of Wen-Lung." I bite back words that would sound peevish and accusing. Keith's heritage—part Anglo, part Indian and part Chinese—had been a sore point with my parents, especially Father.

"You don't think that marrying Keith now will be a problem?" His tone sounds more like a statement than a question.

"Do you still think it's wrong for me to marry someone I love?" He doesn't respond and I press on. "Keith and the kids are my life now, and he is taking care of my children even as we speak. He brings me joy and is faithful to me, while Wen-Lung brought me nothing but heartaches and lies."

Papa's eyes soften and the furrows between his eyebrows ease somewhat. "I'm inclined to believe all you say about Keith, but that doesn't change the fact that he's not Chinese." He sighs and pulls out his favorite chair at the desk. Turning it around, he sits down with a thud, as though weighed down by his burden.

"Why should you let that bother you? All I see is a loving husband and a wonderful father for my children. Keith can't help the fact that he's only half Chinese. What does that matter, anyway? Wen-Lung is completely Chinese, but knowing what you know now, would you have let him marry me?"

"Why couldn't you have found another Chinese man?"

I decide to appeal to the pragmatic side of him. "Don't forget that I'm a divorced woman now, and I also have two small children. Which Hakka man will marry me? Have you looked around to see how many young widows have found a husband here? Keith loves me and my children. Where will I find another man like him?"

"Hmm . . . you and your modern ideas about love and marriage." He pauses, then says gruffly, "If you must marry Keith, then you have my blessings."

Relief courses through my body, and my knees tremble. Although I would have stood up to his disapproval, Father's approval means the world to me. I understand how hard the decision must be for him as an upstanding teacher in this Hakka community of several thousands. By committing to stand by me, he has chosen to swallow his pride and stare down anyone who dares to disrespect that decision.

I want to hug him, but that would be awkward in my family. Instead I touch an arm folded stiffly across his chest. His shoulders drop and he gazes up at me with the hint of a smile. I sit down heavily on a chair beside him. He takes the pictures of Keith and the children from me, grunting and smiling as he shuffles through them.

31

Father hefts a folded cot to his shoulder, brings it into the front room, and then carefully unloads it onto the floor. He unfolds it to reveal a pale yellow canvas. "Maylei, you sleep in the other room with your mother. I've been using your old trundle bed. You can have it now. I'll share this room with your brothers while you're here."

I survey the scene from the narrow hallway where I stand, with a surreal sense of time warp. A jumble of emotions overcome me. Memories of my Toronto home fade away into a distant picture in the mind. On this, my first night in Tangra, the neighborhood tugs at my heart. The stark unpainted walls, cold concrete floors, the absence of anything resembling luxury—these are all beloved.

Father and Kam pull down two cots that lean against the back wall and lay them side by side; the brothers do this every night. Then Father moves the third cot to lie perpendicular at the feet. I go to Mother's room, listen to her shallow breathing, then retrieve the blanket and pillow that lie folded beside her and bring them out for Father.

As children, Jinlei and I had slept on the trundle bed stored underneath the big four-poster one that my parents shared. I used to covet the spare canvas cot because it meant having my own space at night. Mama wouldn't allow me to use it, because then Jinlei would fight me for it. Insignificant details return to me, fragments of memory.

The front door opens and Fu steps inside. He takes his rubber flip-flops off—Mama's house rule number one—and lays them at the side of the doorway before entering. "Maylei Jie Jie, you must find all this quite strange now that you've been away for so long." Even as adults, my brothers still address me as elder sister.

Fu gives me a charming grin. At thirty-two he easily towers over Father by a few inches. Next winter he will marry a Tangra girl and move a few doors down the road. Father and Mother have met the girl and think she will make a good wife for him. Keith and I had originally planned to come for the wedding, but now this unexpected trip will likely change those plans.

"It may be different, but this was my home, where I grew up." I smile. "Are you done for the day?"

Fu pauses in front of me on his way to the bathroom. "Yes, I just finished up at Mr Lee's. I had to measure out the leather to be picked up by a customer tomorrow. By the way, Mr Lee is inviting us all to his place for dinner tomorrow night."

Fu is now Mr Lee's manager. Lately, in addition to overseeing the factory workers, he also does free-lance work tanning rawhide for customers. He wants to rent space at Mr Lee's tannery and go into business for himself.

I can smell a faint odor of leather on him. "That's very kind of him, but we can't all go. Someone has to stay with Ma."

Kam, the youngest of us and always Mother's baby, says, "I'll stay."

I've seen his soft eyes trying to hide his sadness ever since I arrived. I reach for his hand and squeeze it. His lips curl up into the familiar smile. The reserved and shy expression of his face must surely send many a Tangra girl's heart fluttering. He is a Math teacher at Don Bosco's, making him a decent matrimonial catch at twenty-eight.

Father says, "We should ask Jinlei to drop by and stay with your mother instead. She'll be happy to bring her children here to spend some time with their ah-poh."

It's decided.

◆ ◆ ◆

The next evening, Jinlei ushers her two sons and two daughters over. The boys, thirteen and eleven, whoop and jump on the plank bridge across the open sewer between the main road and the tannery.

Inside, Sandy, the youngest, sidles up and tugs at my flared cotton skirt. "Auntie Maylei, Mama says you live in Canada. Where is that?"

I pat her long black hair and tilt her chin up. "It's far, far away. You have to take two airplanes to get there."

Her eyebrows lift with awe. "I've never been on an airplane."

"When I grow up I want to go to Canada too." Barry's voice cracks with pubescent zeal. He is the eldest.

Sandy frowns. "I'm staying here with my mama. I don't want to go far away."

Freddy, number two and not to be outdone, grabs my arm. "Auntie Maylei, take me to Canada with you. I want to see Jay-Son."

I laugh. "Your ma will be very upset with me if I did that."

Jinlei grimaces. "I could use a break, but Freddy, you'll make Mama cry if you leave me now. After you grow up, you can go wherever you want. Come along, you all. Let's go see Ah-Poh."

I follow Jinlei and the children to Mother's bedside. They go up to their grandmother with respectful restraint, gather at her bedside, and speak in hushed tones. The loose skin on Mama's cheeks warbles as she attempts a smile.

Next door Father calls out, "It's time to go to Mr Lee's!"

With another glance at Mother, I take my leave. I pick up Mr Lee's gifts and together with my father and brothers cross the road and enter the big red gate.

32

The Lees' residence is on the second floor of the tannery. This seems to be the new trend, to separate the living space from the work space. Mrs Lee, with eyes creasing into straight lines in her round face, welcomes us into their living room. As soon as he sees us approaching, Mr Lee heaves up from a plush black leather sofa. "Come, come. Sit, sit. Make yourself comfortable in my humble house." He turns to me. "Maylei, ah, how good to see you. How long will you be staying?"

"Not long, two weeks," I reply and sink into a chair.

Mrs Lee calls out to her daughter. "Su-Lan, bring some Campa Cola for our guests."

"No cola, whisky much better." Mr Lee laughs.

Mrs Lee saunters to the wall unit and brings out some glasses and a bottle of Johnnie Walker Red. My brothers and I politely decline; Father and Mr Lee accept the whisky. The rest of us pick up glasses of Indian cola from Su-Lan's tray.

After a brief absence, Su-Lan returns to announce, "Dinner is ready."

We make our way to the inner room, to a round, red Formica-topped table laden with steaming Hakka dishes. Li-Yen, Mrs Lee's eldest daughter-in-law, emerges from the kitchen, smiles and wipes her glistening brow with a handkerchief. She makes a sweeping gesture at the wooden stools circling the table and says, "Please sit."

Through the kitchen doorway I see the backside of a sari-clad maidservant washing pots in a deep sink. Next to her, Li-Yen is now hovering over a wok. I breathe in the pungent aroma of deep-fried chicken sautéed in soya sauce, garlic, onions, and hot pepper—the Hakka way. Turning to Mrs Lee I make the obligatory comment, "You shouldn't have prepared so much food for us."

Mrs Lee responds with a grin and spoons chicken with mushrooms and vegetables into my rice-filled bowl. "Nonsense, I am embarrassed by my paltry table."

I raise a hand to protest. "No more, please." I lift a black mushroom with my chopsticks and sink my teeth into it. "These are truly juicy and delicious."

Her eyes shine with delight. "They're from Hong Kong. I bought them when I visited my sister there last year." She brings her bowl close to her lips and with her chopsticks rapidly scoops up a stream of rice into her mouth.

"And they've been cooked just right."

"You must try one of the shrimp balls." She raises her chopsticks to reach for the golden crisp balls of shrimp and pork, the size of golf balls.

"No, please. Let me." I select one using my chopsticks and balancing it carefully, drop it in my bowl. "I can only cook these occasionally in Canada. Our electric stoves don't get fiery hot like your gas and coal stoves. There's so much open space here. Your cooking smells dissipate quickly."

Mrs Lee agrees. "We are fortunate to have all this space. You people in Canada live in such cramped quarters."

Father and my brothers discuss Tangra politics and business with Mr Lee and two of his three sons. The eldest son, nicknamed Big, holds the half-full bottle of whisky over Father's glass and pours.

Mr Lee says, "The Russians are very interested in my leather."

Fu asks, "The ones that I've been tanning for you?"

Mrs Lee beams at me. "Maylei, thank you for the gifts. You are too generous. Mr Lee and his cronies like a good drink every now and then. Not too much, of course." She wags a finger. "I won't allow them to get drunk in my house."

I hide a smile as I recall Mr Lee passing out on Father's chair holding a half-filled glass. The incident never gets mentioned.

"Mr Lee will get good use of the shirt," Mrs Lee adds.

Su-Lan, a comely young woman, grimaces. "Papa will probably save the shirt and never wear it. He has new clothes that are ancient. When he puts them on, they look like they belong in the nineteenth century."

Mr Lee glares at his daughter beneath his bushy, salt-and-pepper eyebrows. "Unlike you, I don't wear every new outfit right away. I save them for special occasions. You, on the other hand, rush to your tailor with any excuse."

"Well, they don't go out of style the first time I put them on." Su-Lan says, a defiant glimmer in her eyes.

Mr Lee turns to me. "Do you know anyone in Canada who's looking for a wife? Our daughter here seems to enjoy spending my money. It's time she gets married and spends her husband's money instead."

Su-Lan laughs out loud. "Papa, you can't get rid of me that easily. In any case, I'm spending my own money. My teaching salary is quite decent."

"Bah, you're only teaching to pass your time. Girls your age should be married by now."

I turn to Su-Lan. "You are a teacher? I didn't know that!" I throw a meaningful glance at my father and Kam, both teachers.

Mrs Lee elbows me gently. "What's this I hear that you're about to marry an Anglo-Indian?" She looks at my father. "Are you going to let her do that?"

Blank-faced, Father says, "Maylei knows what she wants. We chose her first husband, and look what happened to that marriage. She's a grown woman and can make her own decisions."

Knowing that it's useless to fight these older people who mean well, I maintain a calm demeanor even as Mrs Lee asks, "But can't you find a suitable Hakka man to marry you?"

I don't know whether to laugh or to be angry, and I struggle to erase all emotions from my face. "Mrs Lee, my future husband is half Chinese."

She pats me on my arm. "Yes, dear, I know his mother. What a scandal Lily stirred up when she married an Anglo-Indian. You know it would never have happened had she stayed in the Chinese school with us. But no, she had to go and study English. She thought she was better than the rest of us."

Su-Lan nudges me on the other side. "Excuse my ma, she has old fashioned ideas. You've got it right, Maylei. Marry for love or don't marry at all."

I feel confined, trapped between mother and daughter. I let my gaze fall on Kam. He looks somewhat red-faced and stares away from me into his bowl. It occurs to me that I have been sensing strange vibes between him and Su-Lan this entire evening. I watch for tell-tale signs from Su-Lan. The indignant look she gives her mother seems exaggerated, but her studied avoidance of eye contact with Kam tells me something else.

It saddens me to think that the two will likely never marry, since the Lees' wealth would stand in the way.

Su-Lan pushes her stool back, scraping the concrete floor with a loud squeak. "Can I refill anyone's bowl?"

Mr Lee hands his bowl to her. She turns around and serves him rice from a pot resting on the cupboard behind her.

Mrs Lee says, "Heh, heh, she's really a good girl . . . just very touchy about anything to do with marriage."

Doesn't Mrs Lee see what's going on right under her nose? Maybe she's doing a good job feigning ignorance.

· 33 ·

The wintry morning chill sneaks in through the grill covering the burglar-proof iron bars at the window. It caresses my face, evoking a dreamy reality. Hovering on the edge of wakefulness and sleep, I see Jay-Son and Gracie laughing, Keith chasing them in the park. Suddenly Wen-Lung appears, blocking their way, making Gracie cry. I reach for her, but she slides away from my grasp.

I open my eyes, find myself on the low trundle pull-out. In the dim light, I make out the shape of a heart carved into the side of one leg of my parents' four-poster. I must have been nine or ten when I used a pocket knife to pick at the varnished wood of the leg. Mother had spanked my bottom, and Father had said, "Let her be, there's no harm done." The memory makes me smile. I bring my wrist up to look at my watch. Not yet six o'clock.

"Maylei, are you awake?" I hear Mama's voice, barely audible in the quiet hour. She wants me to sit with her and talk about my life in Canada. "Are you happy?" she asks.

I sit up and begin to fold my covers. "Of course, I am."

"Tell me about Keith. When are you getting married to him?"

I push the trundle bed underneath her bed. "In February."

A deep sigh escapes her lips. "If only I could live long enough to meet your Keith and my new granddaughter."

"Ma, don't worry about the future. I'm here with you right now, and that's all that matters. Keith is with you in spirit. I'll tell Gracie all about you. And Jay-Son, of course he still remembers you, his favorite ah-poh."

Sitting down on her bed, I gently squeeze her gnarled, limp fingers between my palms. Her eyes seem to search my face, perhaps for clues that I'm telling her the truth. "Tell me more about Keith."

"If you met Keith, you'd like him too. Let's see . . . he likes to play soccer, and he's coaching Jay-son's team. He has a good sense of humor. He laughs at my jokes even when they're not funny. He's a very kind and loving man, and he's a good father to my children."

"You were in love with him before we made you marry Wen-Lung." Her tone is sad and wistful. "I'm so sorry."

"Let's not dwell on that now. What matters is that Keith and I are together despite everything." I add, "Ma, I may not have been able to marry Keith all those years ago, but he gave me a part of him that no one could take away from me. Jay-Son is his son."

Ma gives me an angelic smile. "I know. I've always known that Jay-Son wasn't Wen-Lung's son."

"You knew? How? I never told anyone."

"I'm your mother. I knew as soon as I laid eyes on Jay-Son, and he announced he had lungs."

I bring her hand to my lips and kiss it. "Yet you never said a word. Weren't you upset with me?"

She shakes her head with some effort. "How could I be upset at the beautiful baby boy you had brought into this world? If anything, I was disgusted with myself for not letting you marry your sweetheart."

All those wasted years, I think. But deep down, I also realize that I had not put up too much of a fight for Keith. Fatalistically, I had embraced my destiny, believing that fighting my parents was disrespectful and useless.

"What's done is done. I'm happy now. You don't need to worry about me anymore." I knuckle away my tears.

She releases a soft breath. "Go get your father and your brothers."

I hurry next door and call my father and my brothers to join us. With sleepy eyes, they follow me. Father yawns. "Ma, what is it?" He's always addressed Mother as Ma.

"All of you, come closer," Mother whispers.

Fu and Kam shuffle to the foot of the bed while Pa and I sit by her side. A foreboding clutches my heart.

"I want to sit up," Mother says.

Father helps her up, and I prop up pillows behind her.

"My time has come," she says. "No, don't try to deny it. I'm ready to leave anytime now." She closes her eye and it seems she has fallen asleep. I pull her covers over her shoulders. She opens her eyes and gives the shadow of a smile.

"I want to say something." She pauses to take a raspy breath. "I wish I could have more time to see all of you settled down. I wanted to live long enough to see grandchildren from all four of you, but that is not meant to be."

She gazes at Fu. "Fu-Yen, you will get married soon. You will bring a strong woman to replace your worthless mama who doesn't have much breath left. She will look after you like I did."

Fu—distress written all over his face—hunches his shoulders and crosses his arms as if hugging himself. "Ma, you're not going anywhere yet. You'll be here for my wedding." His voice trails off reflecting his own uncertainty.

"Fu-Yen. You know very well that will not happen. Honor your wife the way your father honored me. Look after your father in his old age." Mama turns her attention to Kam now. "I worry about you. If only we could have found you a nice girl too."

Kam shifts from one foot to the other, his eyes on the floor. "Don't worry, Ma. I'll look after myself."

Mother touches Father's hand. "Promise me you will let Kam-Yen marry who he chooses. We made a mistake with Maylei. Let's not repeat that mistake ever again."

"I promise." Father's voice breaks with emotion.

Ma closes her eyes and whispers, "Say goodbye to Jinlei for me. I don't think I can wait long enough for her to come to me."

Father and I carefully help her frail body lie down, rest her head on her pillow, rearrange her covers. I gaze at the peaceful face, pallid and still. Then I note the faint rise and fall of her chest reassuring me that she is still breathing.

There's a banging on our front door. A female voice says, "Can anyone hear me? There's a phone call from Canada."

· 34 ·

Kam and I rush to Mr Lee's place with Su-Lan, who explains that Keith will call back in fifteen minutes. She leads us to the living room where the telephone is located. Was it just last night when we were here drinking and socializing?

The phone rings, and I pick up the receiver.

"Hello, Keith. Has something happened?"

"Maylei?" Keith's voice, metallic and distant. "Wen-Lung has committed suicide; he jumped the Bloor Street bridge over the Don Valley."

"Oh no," I cry out and start to feel my knees buckling. This can't be true. I wished for many things against my ex-husband, but never death. And yet, I shouldn't be surprised given Wen-Lung's previous attempt.

Kam and Su-Lan widen their eyes like large question marks and Kam reaches out a hand to steady me. I gaze at them shaking my head. "When did this happen?" I whisper loudly into the phone.

"This morning, I just received the call from the police. They have your contact information from the last time Wen-Lung tried to commit suicide."

"Does Jay-Son know?" I'm sick to my stomach thinking about how Jay-Son will react to this news. He had nightmares after Wen-Lung's suicide attempt at Centre Island.

"Yes, he knows, he was present when I got the call. That's why I'm calling you. Jay-Son refuses to speak to anyone. He's been in his room ever since he heard the news. Maylei, I'm worried about him."

I hang up the phone and turn wild-eyed to Kam who has been hovering behind me with Su-Lan. He frowns. "What's going on?"

I burst into tears, and he puts his arms awkwardly around me. Su-Lan pats my back, and I can barely explain to them what has happened, my instinct telling me to rush to Toronto this instant. Although I know many self-recriminations will come later, right now my main concern is for my son. Even in my distress I sense the connection between Kam and Su-Lan as they stand beside me, comforting me.

"Let's try calling the airline office now," Kam says.

I'm not hopeful that the office would be open at this early hour, but Su-Lan pulls the massive Calcutta telephone directory from a shelf and begins to thumb through it. She calls out a number as Kam dials. An eternity passes before he hangs up the phone and says, "There's no answer. It's too early. We'll go to the ticket office after breakfast. They'll be open by 9:30."

◆ ◆ ◆

The same morning, Su-Lan and I head off to the city along Chowringhee Road to inquire about my ticket. We are told that the earliest flight available is on Wednesday after midnight. A couple of days from now, not soon enough, but sooner than I expected.

On our way back to Tangra, Park Street is jammed with traffic, and all the cars seem to be honking incessantly. Our driver mutters something about the traffic always being bad. There must be six cars abreast on a road meant for four, with two-wheelers like motorcycles and scooters weaving through the gaps in between.

A Vespa scooter pulls up beside us on Su-Lan's side. A Chinese man looks in at us through the window making wild gestures. I recognize him just as Su-Lan says, "It's Michael. What's he trying to say?"

Su-Lan's cousin, Michael Yap, makes a sign for her to roll down the window. "You better be careful if you're going back to Tangra!" he yells.

She asks, "What's going on?"

" . . . a fight between Chinese and Indians near New Market! The Indians have blocked the roads going to Tangra!"

We happen to be traveling away from New Market. "We're going home," I tell him.

"Keep your eyes open." He threads his scooter between two cars ahead and disappears.

Su-Lan turns to me. "What do you think? Should we stop somewhere and phone home to find out what's going on there?"

I nod. What more can go wrong today? "Let's go to that bookstore down the road, and we'll use the phone. I used to visit it and the owner knew me."

Su-Lan gives the driver directions. "Stupid boys," she mutters. "Hot-headed kids with nothing else to do."

"The fighting is too far to affect us," I reassure her with more composure than I feel.

Mr Bannerjee at the bookstore greets me in Hindi like a long-lost friend. His curly mustache wiggles as he puts his palms together. "Namaste, my daughter. Of course, you can use my phone."

Su-Lan places the call. Her elder brother answers, and she says, "Tai Ko, we're on Park Street. Is it safe for us to come home?" Silence follows and I hold my breath. Then she nods, with a "Tch-tch," and hangs up. "He will call back soon. He's going out to find out what's happening."

We sit on the stools in front of the counter, and soon a man-servant appears with three glasses of steaming chai.

Mr Bannerjee goes away to serve a customer who's brought a list of books to purchase. Half an hour later the phone rings. It's for Su-Lan. Relief comes over her face as she listens on the line. "The roads are clear," she says then, "we can go back now."

Perhaps it's my imagination, but on the way I think I see some young toughs casting hostile glances at us. Our features are obvious. Su-Lan and I unclench our knuckles and breathe easier when we arrive in Tangra without an incident.

· 35 ·

I cross the threshold of our home, and right away I feel the hair on my skin rise. Father, Fu, and Kam all look up as I enter my parents' room. Their faces tell me everything. Without a word I walk over to Mother's bedside. I pick up her lifeless hand—still warm—and bring it to my lips. "Goodbye, Ma. Why didn't you wait for me?" My voice breaks.

I sit on the bed rocking and crying with Mother's hand in mine. Despite all our preparations for this eventuality, her death still takes the wind out of us.

Jinlei calls out from the front room. She must have a sixth sense. One glance at our faces tells her that Mother has passed, and her eyes well up. She uses the bottom of her shirt to wipe her cheeks. Fu brings glasses of water for us, and Jinlei takes charge.

"We need to consult Mr Chang about an auspicious date to bury Ma," she says. She gives directions to both brothers to prepare for Mother's body to be taken to the funeral home. She instructs us about notifying neighbors and relatives. Then she leaves, promising to return soon with a date for the burial.

I finally shake myself out of my stupor when I notice Father visibly shrinking into himself—a mere shadow slumped on the bed—unmoving and pale. Forcefully I blank out thoughts about what's happening back in Canada. Struggling to be calm, I reassert some semblance of control for our present situation. "Papa, come to the other room with me. Let me make you some tea."

In a daze, he lets me lead him by the hand to his usual seat by the desk. Then I go to the kitchen to boil water. As I bring a bowl of tea for Father, there comes the sound of commotion outside on the street. A young Chinese man runs past the front door yelling, "Close your doors, close your doors! The police are coming!"

Someone calls out, "What's going on?"

Another young man comes running behind the first one, and pauses to inform us breathlessly, "An Indian man was killed during the fight. Now the police are arresting any Chinese they meet."

Fu and Kam run to the front door, and they draw the two sides of the latticed iron gate together until they meet in the center. Through the gaps in the lattice we observe more young men tearing down the road. Once Kam has padlocked the gate, Fu closes the wooden door and slides the bolt across to secure the two panels.

I realize that I'm still holding the bowl of tea, paralyzed with fear. An incident like this hasn't happened in a long time. Years ago, a fight broke out when some Chinese teenagers saw a group of Indian youths taunting a Hakka girl outside New Market near Nizam Restaurant in central Calcutta. Lots of glass bottles were thrown and broken, and knives were bared and flailed. Fortunately no one was killed.

The Hakka community has a healthy distrust of the police, who come to Tangra every now and then to wield their authority and arrest a young man or two. No one wants to be nearby when they are out hunting for a scapegoat. The best course of action is to hide, preferably outside Tangra, before they arrive.

I put my bowl of tea on the desk and sit down on a chair beside Father to stop my trembling knees from buckling. I mutter a prayer to no one in particular, "Please don't let this trouble last. We have to bury Mama and I have a flight to catch."

Father sips the tea and mumbles, "Did you get your flight confirmed?"

"Yes. I'm leaving in a couple of days."

He sips again and puckers his brow, regaining some of his old self. "These hot-headed youngsters always cause trouble for us."

Kam clenches his jaws. "The cops can't come here arresting everyone just because we're Chinese."

Father sits up, squares his shoulders. "The two of you, stay away from the police. I don't want them to catch you."

I see the tension and worry on his face. The lines on his forehead and his cheeks have deepened. Mother's illness and now her death have ravaged him.

Fu paces the floor. "We have to be ready to run out the back should the police come knocking."

The possibility sickens me. "I pray that this won't happen. Maybe the white cloth over our door will warn them that someone has died here and they'll leave us alone."

Kam laughs mirthlessly. "They're Indians. They don't know what that white cloth means."

"Well, if they come, I will tell them."

Sirens wailing. When they cease, snatches of conversations in Bengali—indiscernible and harsh-sounding—and we strain to hear what they are saying. Suddenly our iron gate rattles.

I glance at my brothers. Fu whispers urgently, "Come, Kam, let's go out the back way now."

My heart hammering inside me, I follow them as they rush out. The sound of metal rattling outside is now accompanied by something beating on the wooden door through the latticed iron door. *"Darwaja kholo!"* someone bellows outside in Hindi for us to open the door.

I quickly lock the back door after my brothers. Returning to the front, I make a lot of noise unbolting the long wooden bar. Easing one door panel a few inches out, I say, "There's only me, my old father and my dead mother in here. My mother just passed away."

A dark mustachioed face peers through the gap. "Open the door. We want to come inside."

"Please Bhai, what have we done? We are mourning my mother's death."

"Then let us see for ourselves." The mustache quivers.

I glance back at Father as he shuffles toward me. "Please leave us alone," I plead.

"Where are the men in your home?"

"Only my father lives here with my mother. I'm visiting them."

"Then you don't have to be afraid. Open up."

Taking a deep breath, I slowly pull open one panel. Now with just the latticed gate between us, I see another policeman beside the first one. Their wooden lathis swing menacingly by their sides.

I compose my face into the saddest expression I can muster. "You can see there's just me and my old father. We are both in mourning. My dead mother is inside. Can't you leave us out of respect for her?"

"Let us see for ourselves," says the mustachioed officer.

I pick up the keys from the table and with deliberate care I remove the lock on the gate. The two officers push the gate open. They head straight for Mother's room. Within a few seconds they return ashen-faced.

"Let's get out of here," one man says to the other. They can't go out fast enough, thumping on the wooden plank with extra zeal as they cross the open sewer.

Father and I sit in tense silence for a while after the cops have left. Soon he rises from his chair, clasps his hands behind him, and starts to pace.

"Papa, everything will be all right. Ma is looking after us wherever she is now . . . and I'm sure it's a good place where she no longer feels pain."

He stops to look at me. "Bad things happen for a reason . . . I know that. And I also know that we're supposed to learn lessons from them. It's just that when they're happening to us, sometimes it's hard to see anything positive. Maylei, you must sponsor us to come to Canada when you go back."

"I will do that, Papa."

A noise at the back startles us. Father stands still and I hold my breath as we listen to the soft knocking sounds.

"Papa, Maylei? It's Fu and Kam."

◆ ◆ ◆

A day after Mother's funeral, I arrive in Toronto with a mixture of relief, concern, and overwhelming guilt. The long flight home gave me plenty of time to process my feelings. Jay-Son will be fine; I spoke to Keith again before I left Calcutta. But what about me? My past is forever intertwined with Wen-Lung. His final leap was a desperate response to his inability to deal with his problems. Yet even as I rail at his selfish act, I realize that I am trapped in my own prison of doubts and self-blame. His demons are now my shame. In time I will learn to forgive myself. I must.